The House at Akiya

The House at Akiya

WILLIAM BUTLER

New York   CHARLES SCRIBNER'S SONS

To Elinore

AUTHOR'S NOTE

I have made some very minor amendments in this book since its original publication in England, and shall hope in some very minor way to have improved it. I should like also to explain that the book had originally, if privately, a different title, a Japanese title: *Akiya-no-akiya*, and the "feeling" of this title, in Japanese, conveys a rather more sensitive idea than its direct translation ("The Empty House at Akiya") offers. The "feeling" is more closely adhered to in the simpler title under which the book is published. *Akiya*, according to the characters used, can be read to mean "autumn valley" (in fact, the name of the town) or "empty house," while the Japanese postposition *no* indicates possession ("of" or "at"), and a peculiarly sensitive depth is felt in the combining of the two words, something more than the literal statement of "the empty house," which is in fact *too* literal: thus, the abbreviated English title. In a sense, the difference might be measured by the meaning of the word "house" as read, in the title, first before, and then after, reading the novel. Some portion of this alteration of "feeling" is already inherent in the Japanese title.

W.B.

The
House at
Akiya

1

Not long after taking the house in Akiya, neighbours had informed Ephraim Rome and his wife that a young man and young woman had only recently committed suicide there. They had taken poison together. Mrs Rome was horrified, but Ephraim only smiled a bit and said that Americans were more practical about affairs of the heart. He certainly saw no reason to move, even though his wife hinted that it might not be such a bad idea, and he grew irritable if she as much as alluded to it.

'Look here,' he told her, 'it had nothing to do with the house. It had only to do with the absence of cool sensibilities. I have no intention of surrendering my good sense simply because a couple of kids I never met surrendered theirs. Now, let's hear no more about it.'

One day, however, a neighbour informed Mrs Rome that it hadn't been senseless passion so much as discouragement; the couple had no longer been able to afford the house at Akiya, and the wife had been pregnant and, to bring the matter to its insoluble head, the young man was in trouble with his employers. It had not been passion, but defeat, which led them to die in that house.

'I didn't want to move down here in the first

13

place,' Mrs Rome told Ephraim one night. 'I wish we could have stayed in Tokyo. In fact, I wish we could go back to America.'

'If there was anyone anxious to get out of Tokyo into the country, it was you, you know,' her husband reminded her. 'And if I were to ask to be returned to the States, I'd have pretty much ruined my chances for getting where I want to go with this organization. You know that, too. And since you were the one who wanted to live out of the city, as we lived out of New York, I don't see why—'

'But I didn't ask to be stuck in a haunted house, either,' retorted Mrs Rome.

'Are you really going to plague me with a word like "haunted"?'

'Well, it makes me nervous to be here. And I don't think the children like it, either.'

'Why?' asked Ephraim. He had noticed nothing at all in either the eight-year-old boy or the five-year-old girl to indicate anything but pleasure with the house. It was right by the sea, which they loved, and the air was much better than in Tokyo.

'I don't know why,' said Mrs Rome. 'I only know that they seem edgy. They seem *different* down here.'

'It's a different place. Why shouldn't they seem different? So far as I can see, they're happy here, and for the last time, let's make this an end of the whole discussion.'

Ephraim felt that he himself had the most to complain about so far as living in Akiya was concerned. It was he who had to travel an hour and a half into

14

Tokyo and an hour and a half home five days each week—three hours of daily commuting—and it was impossible to shave the time any closer. He tried leaving his bus at Zushi Kaigan and taking a little red and yellow shuttle train into Kanazawa Hakkei to board the Shinagawa express, but that was no faster than taking the Yokosuka Line train from Zushi Station.

The only answer for so much commuting time was to do some of the reading Ephraim had for years told himself he ought to do, and so he left the office one afternoon and went into Nihombashi to visit the Maruzen store. There he purchased a number of books by Japanese writers, in order to help familiarize himself with the nature of the country in which he was living.

First he read a short book of poems, unusual for him because he didn't care for poetry at all, but it was the shortest book he had bought and thus the most attractive with which to begin. Included were a number of poems by an ancient poet named Hitomaro, lamenting the death of Hitomaro's wife.

His own wife discovered the book in his pocket one day and read the poems with wonder. 'Why,' she asked him when the children were in bed, 'are you reading that book? You don't like poetry.'

'Well, I've got to do *something* while I'm on the train for an hour. What else is there to do but read?'

'But you're reading poems.'

He shrugged.

'Ephraim,' she said, 'do you like those poems?'

15

He thought about it and said, 'I suppose they're pretty. I certainly have no way of judging whether poetry is good.'

'But they're very gloomy, some of them.'

'I suppose poets are generally gloomy people, aren't they?'

'And then, those Hitomaro poems,' she said.

'Which ones were those?'

'The one about the dead wife.'

'Oh yes. Very interesting,' although Ephraim wasn't sure why he said so. If a man was a poet, it should be reasonable enough that he would write poems about his dead wife.

'Ephraim, doesn't it seem even a little strange to you to find yourself suddenly reading poems about a dead wife?'

'No, it doesn't. Why? Are you thinking about that couple again? Good God, but you're morbid. There's certainly no relationship between the fact that I've begun to do a little reading on the train and the troubles those people had. I thought we were done with that subject.'

'All right, Ephraim,' murmured Mrs Rome, and she said no more about the poems.

For a few days, Ephraim restricted his reading to American magazines and English-language newspapers, but then he picked up another of the books he kept at his office and began to read it on the train. It seemed to be a short historical novel, though for a time he couldn't be certain whether it was fiction or history. It seemed there had been a battle between two great clans in ancient times and the Emperor, a mere child, was one of the victims. His nurse had leaped with him into the sea to prevent his being captured and slain by the enemy. A great force of men were lost at sea and it was said that the curious crabs which inhabited that area were the ghosts of the men killed in battle. When he finished reading the opening chapters of the book, Ephraim still didn't know whether the book was history or fiction.

At home that night, he learned that his son, Carl, had had a slight accident; his thumb was bandaged and the boy's eyes were still wet from crying.

'A crab bit me,' complained the boy.

'Probably a ghost,' grinned Ephraim, tugging at Carl's ear.

Mrs Rome was startled. 'Why did you say that?'

Ephraim looked at his wife quizzically. 'No reason. Oh, I was reading a book on the train. There was some sort of a sea battle, and superstition had it that the ghosts of the dead appeared in the form of crabs. That's all. But it doesn't seem as though the ghosts were able to do much damage to Carl, does it?'

'He bit me,' said Carl. 'I picked him up and pretty soon he bit me.'

'It was a teeny little crab,' said Nancy, the girl, 'and it wasn't a very bad bite. I wanted one too, but I couldn't find one, so that crab just bit Carl.'

The next morning, Saturday, Ephraim found his wife reading the book he had brought home. 'Maybe you can tell me,' he smiled at her, 'whether that thing is a story or a text? I'm damned if I know.'

17

His wife shook her head. 'It's a warning,' she muttered.

Ephraim chuckled, though he didn't understand her.

'Ephraim, we must leave this house,' his wife said with sudden passion.

'Why?'

'There are spirits here.'

'Oh, stop it.'

'Ephraim, there's something wrong with this house.'

'Stop it!'

His wife would not stop, and began to plead with Ephraim to find a new house in Tokyo, and when he discouraged her in that, reminding her of all the trouble it had been to move from Tokyo to Akiya, she began to plead with him to leave the country altogether, to return to America. 'These spirits are hostile to us,' she cried, 'they don't want us here.'

'You've never been like this before,' he told her. 'What's come over you? Do you really believe in ghosts?'

'I don't believe in anything,' she said wretchedly. 'I only know that something is wrong, and I'm unhappy here, and so are the children.'

'If they're unhappy here, it's because you're making them unhappy.'

'Ephraim, let's go back to America.'

'That's impossible, and you know it.'

'Let's go home!'

'It's out of the question! Now go to bed and leave me alone.'

2

Ephraim took the children for a walk on Sunday. They walked along by the sea, hopping over the great rocks which jutted into the shore, around the one mountainous rock which stood ghostly at the edge of the sea, trailing across the narrow strips of sand, stooping to watch the little sea animals in the brilliantly clear water.

'There's a crab, like the one that bit me,' called Carl from one rock, and Ephraim hurried over to watch the little creature speed sideways across the rock. It was white and rose-hued, with traces of dull green about its antennae; it was not difficult to understand how such a weirdly beautiful thing might be taken for a ghost, particularly if it were much larger, such as the crabs were said to have been where the sea-battle had taken place towards the Southern end of Honshu. The crab vanished into a little cave-like hole in the rock and Ephraim walked on with the children.

They were sitting on the sand, enjoying the warmth of the sun, when Ephraim all at once realized the children were speaking Japanese together.

'What are you saying?' he asked Carl.

'Oh, we're just talking,' Carl said in English.

'Are you really speaking Japanese?'

'E, so desu,' said the little girl. 'Chichi wa, hana-shimasen, hanashimasen,' and she laughed shrilly, and Carl laughed with her.

'Well, what was that about?' smiled Ephraim.

'I won't tell you, I won't tell you,' shrieked the girl.

'It isn't very nice to keep secrets from your father,' said Ephraim.

The children laughed, and Carl began to say, 'Baka baka baka, chichi wa baka ni sareru no wa iya desu!'

Carl laughed alone, Nancy gazing at him inquiringly, and then she added, 'Chichi wa, futotta baka desu ne?' Carl laughed freshly, and that seemed to please Nancy, who began to laugh again, herself.

Ephraim chuckled but began to feel nervous and he took the children back along the beach to the house.

'Well,' he told his wife over lunch, 'these kids seem to be picking up Japanese very quickly. I wonder if they're really saying something, or just imitating syllables.'

'They're making sense, all right,' said Mrs Rome, 'and it makes me uneasy. They refuse to speak two languages at the same time, it's one or the other, and they'll never tell you what they say in the other.'

'So I notice. Well, I guess we'd better start studying ourselves, or we'll wind up losing our own children.'

'That's not a very nice way of putting it,' his wife seemed genuinely upset.

'Oh, good God,' snapped Ephraim, and he stood up from the table and left the room.

In the evening, seated behind the house and gazing at the darkening water, he heard the voices of his children from the street, singing together:

> 'Toryanse, toryanse . . .
> Koko wa doko no hoso michi ja?'

His daughter was having definite trouble with both the words and the tune, but his son's voice carried clearly, even prettily, around the house, seeming to Ephraim to sing the foreign song all too easily:

> 'Ikiwa yoi yoi kaeri wa kowai . . .
> Kowai nagara mo,
> To-oh-ryan-se . . . toryanse . . .'

Ephraim stood up as a small man in a rumpled hat with a cigarette dangling from his mouth came along the beach. The man bowed to Ephraim and Ephraim nodded his head in return. 'Good evening,' said Ephraim.

'Good evening,' said the man with a grin, his English satisfactory.

'Do you live hereabouts?'

'Ah, I beg pardon?'

'Do you live near here?'

'Ah, yes yes, I do. There,' he gestured back in the direction from which he came.

'Then we're neighbours,' said Ephraim, and he gave the man his hand. The Japanese put his hand out and let Ephraim shake it a bit before withdrawing it. 'My name is Rome.'

The man nodded. 'How do you do? I am Inoue. How do you do?'

'Say,' said Ephraim, 'can you tell me what those kids are singing about?'

'Kids?'

'Well, the children,' he motioned towards the street. 'The song. What is it?'

'Ah, that is song about Japanese holiday, *Shichi-go-san*, you know? Children go to shrine. Dress up. Very beautiful.'

'But where would my kids learn a song like that? My children?'

'Is it true? These are your children? Your wife, Japanese?' The stranger seemed astonished.

'No, my wife is American. I can't understand how they learned so quickly. The kids. The children.'

'And you have been here for a long time? In Japan?'

'Just a half year or so. Six months.'

'So short? I see.' The man took in his breath, grinned and shook his head. 'Your children learn so fast. I could not tell them from Japanese children.'

'What do the words mean? Can you really understand them?' asked Ephraim.

'Very clear, very clear, very fine. Yes, song says how children go to shrine, to Tenjin, but very uncertain about . . . very uncertain about, whether outcome is what is wanted, you understand? Song says, must be brave and go through, even though

22

not knowing what happens.' The man chuckled awkwardly. 'My English so bad, excuse me. Song says not important. Just Japanese song, Japanese holiday. Your children, very fine Japanese. Very good.'

The two parted and Ephraim listened to the children sing the song again and was intrigued by the children's ability to adopt not only the new language, but what must have been even new meanings, so swiftly.

3

The next morning, on the train, Ephraim tried to read a newspaper, but couldn't concentrate upon it. He kept thinking of the children's new outlook, for it seemed to him that with the new language and new meanings they were adopting a new way of seeing and thinking, and he thought of their secrecy with these things. He tried to recall the song the children had been singing, but he could not.

That afternoon he received a telephone call from Akiya with the news that his son had died in the sea that morning.

It was not the sort of news from which he could pick himself up and rush home. He sent his secretary from his office and wept upon his desk. If the call had told him that Carl had been hurt, then he would have taken himself home without delaying even to button his collar, but to be told so bluntly, by the maid who made the call for his wife, that his son was dead—there was no energy in him to move.

What had made the boy go into the sea? Carl couldn't swim at all. Grief crowded close about him, overwhelmed him, and sound and light charged in on him, then vanished; and uncontrollably, the song his son had sung touched his mind—never certainly, but in phases, in knowledge more than in melody. Finally, he brought his senses together and left his office, to return to Akiya.

He walked to Tokyo Station. Curiously drained of any desire to hurry home, he kept walking into Kyobashi, through the Ginza and finally into Shimbashi.

He stopped at a small bar and had a whisky and scowled at the girl who smiled at him from the dark shadows across the room. He left the bar and walked to Shimbashi Station, and waited there for a train. When he saw a girl smiling near him, he had the irrational thought that it was the girl who had watched him from the shadows of the bar. He scowled and snapped, 'Are you following me?'

The girl, frightened, hurried away from him and Ephraim saw that it was certainly not the same girl.

When he arrived home, his wife began to cry. 'I told you,' she cried, 'I told you, I told you, and you wouldn't leave this house.' She would speak only of the house and was still more dazed than Ephraim, it seemed, for she wasn't prepared to speak of the boy's death in any direct manner, but only to look upon it as having been an inevitability.

Ephraim spoke with a neighbour, a woman he had never seen before, and the woman couldn't look him in the eyes as she tearfully told him what had happened in her halting English. The boy had tried to climb a mountainous rock at the side of the sea, having seen a Japanese boy succeed at the same thing. The Japanese boy had been smaller than Carl, and there had been something in the nature of a challenge. It was a dangerous ascent and Carl simply couldn't complete it. He fell into the sea and against its sharp rocks.

It was useless for Ephraim to hunt after words. There was nothing to say.

'Brave boy,' said the woman after a time, still tearfully unable to face Ephraim. 'Brave boy, sing, then die.'

'Sing?' Ephraim repeated. 'Singing a song? After he fell?'

'Brave boy, good boy,' and the woman lost her ability to speak and turned away.

Nancy had been taken to the neighbour's house to play with the children there and it was only later that night that she learned her brother had been hurt and would not return to play with her.

Nancy didn't cry. She gave no indication of needing to cry. She only gaped with what seemed to Ephraim an odd and even frightening kind of knowledge, and she said, 'I wonder where he is, though.'

Nancy went to bed that night and had trouble sleeping, but she didn't cry at all. She simply stared and seemed thoughtful and didn't appear to react to, or need, the comforting hand which Ephraim kept upon her until she dropped off.

The boy's funeral was held two days later in Yokohama, and again Nancy was left with the neighbours. After the funeral, nothing was said by Ephraim or Mrs Rome until they were back in the house at Akiya.

Then Ephraim said, 'Perhaps you were right. Perhaps there *is* something unlucky for us about this house. I think we may as well give it up.'

But his wife shook her head.

Ephraim could scarcely believe her gesture. 'Surely you don't want to stay here?'

'Ephraim,' she said, 'now it doesn't matter. The thing has begun.'

'What are you talking about? What has begun?'

'They didn't want us here and I felt it. I warned you. But there isn't anything to be done about it now. Once they've begun, they won't stop.'

'Won't stop what? Who won't stop? What's the matter with you?'

His wife didn't answer.

'You actually want to stay here?' he asked her in still deeper disbelief.

'Do you know that Carl was singing just before he died?'

'I know it.'

'Mrs Nakano told me. It was a song about being brave and doing what one had to do.'

'*Toryanse*,' muttered Ephraim.

Mrs Rome stared at him. 'You know the song?'

'It's only a song about a children's holiday. What if he was singing it?'

'I don't know,' she replied vacantly, turning from him. 'I don't know why I brought it up. But this is where he . . . somehow, it's as if he might still be . . . here.'

'Good God,' he growled at her.

'I don't want to go from here, Ephraim.'

'Good God,' he said, 'first you wanted to get out because you were afraid of ghosts, and now you want to stay in order to create a ghost. You were right, I tell you. This place is no good for us. We'll have to move.'

'No.'

'But I say yes!'

'I won't go, Ephraim. I really won't.'

He argued with her, but she was as set upon remaining as he was upon leaving.

He was angry and left the house and took the train to Tokyo, thinking to go to the office, but he realized as he rode through the towns of thatch and tiled roofs and the wet paddies that he couldn't think of working yet. He thought of Carl, of how young his son had been, and then had to force his thoughts away in order to ease the aching of his throat. He left the train at Shimbashi and walked about for a time and, when he passed the bar he had visited on Monday, he quickened his step.

And yet he passed the bar many times, eventually going into it, as if drawn there by his recollection and wanting to live as much in the house of his sorrow as his wife. He took the same stool he had taken on Monday and ordered a whisky, then began to watch for the girl who had been there. There was a girl, but he wasn't certain she was the same girl, and when she stood up to leave, he looked at her questioningly; she smiled. He simply couldn't remember what the girl had looked like, and decided that this was the girl, and he felt like talking to her, as if because she had shared his afternoon of supreme sorrow, however obscurely.

'Hello,' he ventured, unable to return her smile.

'Oh, hello,' she said in a kind of casually sensual manner; it would not be difficult to speak with her.

'Do you speak English?'

'Oh, I speak some English. Very badly, excuse me. And do you speak Japanese?' She had come over to sit beside him, backwards, leaning against the bar. She was neither beautiful nor unattractive. Her features were not fine enough to be beautiful, and yet there was still more than the beauty of youth in her face, some of it so plain as to be wanton. 'You are an American.'

'Maybe I'm English.'

'Maybe you are American,' she said, and laughed.

'Well,' Ephraim asked in a moment, fingering his glass, 'why don't you sit with me for awhile? Let me buy you a drink.'

'Oh yes. I like drinks,' and she turned around on her stool and smiled at the young barman. He needed no instructions to prepare her drink. It was green. 'Now,' she said, lifting the drink, 'here is to America and Japan.'

She sipped and when she set the glass down, Ephraim picked it up and, while she tried to retrieve the glass tasted it. The drink was mint-flavoured water.

'Marvellous,' Ephraim set the glass down.

'Do you mind?' she asked with a mixture of brazenness and coyness which displeased Ephraim.

'Is it terribly expensive?' Ephraim asked, trying to smile but failing.

The girl laughed. 'Your drink is not water. Why not drink it, be happy?'

'And then buy you another? And then be charged two or three thousand yen—that will include the mint flavouring, of course—and then you will say goodbye, and return later to get your thousand yen? Yes, I should be happy. All the world is a place for happiness. You make me very happy.' He was trying to think of something vicious to tell the girl, but his mind wouldn't work at it.

Again she laughed. 'You must not say such things.'

'Oh, I must. I must.' Ephraim gave her a piece of a smile but it was not a real smile, it was bitterness and contempt, and he began to wonder if he had been looking for someone only against whom he might hurl these unexpected emotions. He drank from his whisky and tried to settle himself. 'I am only distracting myself. I'm writing a poem. Like Hitomaro. Except I'm lamenting the death of my son. And except that I'm writing mine in green water and whisky. Now, I wonder if you understand?'

'No,' she smiled, 'I do not understand you.'

'My son died this week. Carl. My son. We buried him in Yokohama this week. In the ground. And so it's time for poetry. Not being a poet, I'm drinking with you. A man must be a poet as best he knows how.'

She seemed not to know whether to smile or stop smiling. She blinked at him.

'What is your name?' Ephraim asked the girl. 'I need details for my poem. I wish to know your parentage, your schooling, your profits, everything. We'll start with your name.'

'My name is Saeko.'

'Is that all?'

'Just Saeko,' she smiled but less brazenly than before.

'Saeko. Very well, it will have to do. Saeko, are you married?'

'No,' she giggled but vaguely.

'Then you have no children.'

Her discomfort seemed to grow.

'Well, Saeko,' Ephraim said, unsure whether he was trying to make vicious talk or just useless talk, 'do you like poetry?'

'I do not know.'

'Don't you like Hitomaro? Why, all women like Hitomaro. Hitomaro liked women, and women liked Hitomaro. Isn't he a friend of yours?'

'My friend? Oh, no.'

'Hitomaro, Hitomaro,' muttered the barman, nodding. He wiped a glass and smiled at Ephraim. It seemed that it was the one word of the conversation he had understood.

'All right, Saeko,' said Ephraim, 'do you know about the great sea-battle in which the Emperor Antoku died? How old was he? Seven?'

'I don't know,' she admitted, gazing into her mint-coloured drink.

'Why, I know more about Japan than you do,'

said Ephraim. 'You aren't really Japanese at all. You're Chinese. Isn't that right? You're a spy. Do you know the song, *Toryanse?*'

'Oh, yes,' she sighed, smiling, but there was nothing cheerful about her smile.

'What does it mean?'

'*Toryanse?* Oh, is only a song, you know. No important meaning, I think.'

'But it means a child must go into life, doesn't it? Must go through with life? Life is a God-damned commitment, isn't that it? It means to be brave.'

She looked at him at last, studying his face. 'Is it true? Did your little boy die?'

Ephraim was taken by surprise and looked away, then nodded.

She shook her head. 'I am sorry.'

He shrugged, not certain how he should accept sympathy and not wanting any, but the shrug had felt too callous a gesture and he looked down and mumbled, 'Thank you.'

The girl addressed the barman, speaking in Japanese, and the young man wiped at his glasses more slowly, gazing at Ephraim briefly, then turning away without answering the girl.

'I'm sorry,' it was now Ephraim who felt extreme discomfort. 'I shouldn't be bothering you.'

'I wonder what I can do?' said the girl in a moment, and she seemed so impulsively sincere that once again Ephraim was taken off guard.

'There's nothing you can do, of course. Forgive me for speaking of it to you.'

32

'How,' she began, then waited, then finished her sentence, 'how did that little boy die?'

'He fell from a rock. Over the sea. He died singing your *Toryanse*.'

'Is it true?' For what seemed a long time she was silent, and then she again spoke to the barman in Japanese, interrupting herself to tell Ephraim in English: 'Brave boy. Your boy was brave.'

The barman, glancing obliquely at Ephraim, said something in a quiet voice, mentioning the name Antoku.

Saeko turned to Ephraim. 'He says how he understand why you speak of child Emperor Antoku, who also die in the sea.' She kept looking at Ephraim and seemed to be restraining tears, and Ephraim had a sudden wish to take her hand and comfort her, but he resisted it.

'Now I must go,' Saeko said. 'Please forgive me.' She stood up and without another word, she hurried from the bar, Ephraim wondering at the speed of her departure.

It must have been, he decided, that she wished to weep, that he had made her miserable. He spent some more time over his whisky, paid the barman without being charged for the girl's water nor overcharged for his drinks, and he left the bar.

Outside, it was dark. The glare of Shimbashi's neon-lighted streets somehow emphasized the distance between himself and Akiya, and Ephraim felt lonely. He began to walk about the streets and finally went into a tiny restaurant and ordered *yaki-*

tori without knowing what he was ordering. He ate the chicken with a large cup of hot *sake* and felt refreshed, not noticing the curious glances of the Japanese patrons of the cafe.

He walked to Shimbashi Station and took the train to Zushi, then the green and yellow bus to Akiya.

His wife was awake when he came into the house and she told him the maid had quit her job that day. There had been no proper reason for it but she said she had bad feelings about the house, and Mrs Rome told Ephraim she could well understand the maid's feelings.

'And what about you?' he asked. 'Wouldn't you rather leave.'

She didn't answer, but instead asked: 'Where have you been?'

'Tokyo. Walking around.'

'Did you eat?'

'Yes, I had something.'

'Will you try to find a new maid?'

'I'll inquire for you, yes,' he said, 'but I wish you'd let me take a place in Tokyo.'

'I'm just not up to moving now,' and she turned over and away from him.

4

The following week Ephraim returned to work.

It was difficult. His personal life was far from settled. He was worried about Nancy, the little girl, for she missed her brother, yet didn't cry and didn't complain. The child mooned about and seemed to be searching for a way of enjoying life without Carl to guide her. It wasn't much better with his wife; she too had little to say, and had grown touchy about moving, so much so that Ephraim didn't like bringing up the subject at all. Yet she wasn't happy at Akiya, and with Nancy so silent and his wife so distracted, Ephraim preferred not to be at the house.

He began to work harder at unnecessary things, since such work both kept him at the office and focused his attention upon painless objects. When his wife complained of his increasingly late hours, he told her it was a busy season and there was nothing he could do about it, and instead of coming home earlier he began to return even later.

There seemed less and less to talk about with his wife each day, for her thoughts were fast upon the nature of her own misery; she talked about strange things, too, which he couldn't understand, speaking sentences which seemed incomprehensible, and all of these things he related to her feeling about the house that she wouldn't leave. He had the feeling that the house had in some way captured his wife, imprisoned her, that it nearly was as if spirits, malicious and dominant, inhabited it.

One evening Ephraim returned to the bar in Shimbashi, to the place where he had relaxed his first remorse, and he wondered if he would see Saeko there. Her sympathy had been, if unwelcome, at least rational, and he had the strange feeling that he shared something with that girl. He did not see her that evening, and it bothered him. The barman remembered him and smiled at him, but Ephraim had not come to see the barman and, after an hour and three whiskys, he left the bar.

He returned to the same bar the next night, hoping to see Saeko, finding it odd in himself that he was now consciously looking for a girl who, being pretty and being young, he might have been seeking for just those reasons; but he had the feeling that Saeko knew him and could speak to him, and that he knew her and could speak to her. He didn't trust the feeling, but made no effort to dispel it. He had seen her dishonesty, she had seen his lament; he accepted it as a kind of mutual knowledge. Saeko did not come, and Ephraim left.

The following week he encountered the girl at the bar and she was with a young Japanese man, far better-looking than Ephraim and, he supposed, surely more attractive to Saeko. For no good reason, he was incensed and pretended he did not recognize her. She said, 'You do not remember? I am sorry,' and she went to sit at a little table with her friend.

36

Later she came again to sit beside him and said, 'Excuse me, I trouble you. I sit with you one day, you are unhappy. Now you cannot remember, and I apologize.'

'Listen, Saeko,' he told her, feeling the moving presence of whisky within his brain, 'I remember you. You understand? Therefore, *I* apologize to you. Now we have both been courteous. What comes next?'

She didn't look as though she understood. 'I wish to say something to you. I did not think to see you again, but I go to shrine, pray for your son. I did.'

'Shrine?' Through the whisky, Ephraim tried to connect a shrine to his present situation. 'Shrine . . . Tenjin-sama, Tenjin-sama. Well?'

'Yes, Tenjin-sama. You understand? Your son sang song *Toryanse*, isn't it true? I go to shrine for him.'

'Oh, I see,' Ephraim woke up a little, then looked unclearly into the girl's eyes. 'Who are you with?'

'I am with friend, my good friend,' she said. She motioned to her friend, which irked Ephraim, but the young man came over. 'This is my friend, Yoshio. He does not speak English.'

Ephraim shook hands with the young man, eyeing him gloomily as Saeko spoke to him in Japanese.

'He says,' Saeko translated, 'can he buy you drink?'

'Oh, no,' smiled Ephraim, too suddenly becoming aware of the girl's youth. She was, he had realized, young, but he hadn't tried to think it out. Standing beside the boy, perhaps fifteen or more years his junior, he saw that Saeko might have been as young as seventeen or eighteen. Some aspect of his own morality swam amidst the whisky in his brain and he became embarrassed and stood up.

'Well, it was good to meet you,' he told the youth thickly, and he nodded to Saeko. 'Goodbye. Thanks for the prayer.'

5

That night, after he arrived home, Ephraim told his wife he was going to wire the home office about being returned to America.

'No no,' his wife grew excited and Ephraim was bewildered. 'No, not now. Ephraim, we can't leave him here. This is where he *is*.'

'Are you talking about Carl? For God's sake, will you just try to be sane about what has happened? Carl is dead. We've lost him! And we've got to get away from here before we're worse off than he is. Do you understand?'

'Don't talk like that,' she shook her head violently. 'I won't go, Ephraim. I want to stay here.'

Nothing he could say would relieve his wife of her excitement, and it was useless trying to talk to her.

Ephraim left the house and walked down by the sea's sifting corners and stared back at the house in the moonlight. It was a beautiful thing to see. It was not a large house, but the paper screens softened the harsher light within and the shadows seemed infected with the night colour of the water itself, and a kind of sea light seemed to fall rhythmically from the moon to hold the house gently in its evening grasp; it was as if the Japanese house had made some

39

pact with nature. The house looked as if it were something not which had been built, but which had grown there. At the same time, it was a kind of prison and Ephraim, gazing at the house, couldn't be sure whether he was adoring it or despising it.

He looked down the beach to the giant rock, where Carl had climbed, had fallen. The tide was in and the sea slipped about and licked at the base of the gigantic rock, and the moonlight reflected itself in its wet orange sides. 'How can we stay here?' Ephraim whispered aloud. He was growing convinced that his wife had become rather unbalanced by the tragedy, for otherwise she ought really to be more anxious than ever to leave. He stared at the rock, whispering, 'We can't stay here.'

But by remaining at the house at Akiya, by not mentioning his own distrust of the place, Ephraim found that he could live somewhat more peaceably with his wife. She didn't bring up such absurdities as spirits, nor issue so many wholly incomprehensible mutterings, so long as he steered clear of any word about leaving or about the tragedy. It began to be as though Carl had never existed. Avoidance of his name and of the topic of moving seemed poor comfort to Ephraim, however, for his work hours only grew later and later, and on occasion he was at his office all night in preference to returning to observe his stoic wife or his cheerless daughter at silent play.

One night, by sheerest coincidence, he ran into Saeko. He had walked into Nishiginza to take dinner and she had been window-shopping.

40

'Oh, hello,' she said. 'Do you remember me? How are you?'

'Hungry,' he smiled heavily. He watched her for some seconds, then added, 'I wonder . . . are you also hungry?'

'Hungry?' She pursed her lips into a curious smile, apparently not understanding the purpose of his question. 'I will eat at home, though. I hope your wife, she is better now?'

'Oh, yes,' he looked away. 'Look, I was just going to dinner.' For some reason it was hard being direct with her, but he at last managed, 'I wish you would be hungry away from home.'

'Away? Oh, you mean to have my dinner, and you, together?'

'I wish you would. I was just walking over to Mikasa Kaikan. Why not go along with me?'

'Oh, yes,' she smiled. 'All right. Thank you.'

The simplicity of her willingness somehow tended to re-emphasize her youth to Ephraim, as if she trusted him all too easily, and he felt a little embarrassed as they walked up the stairs to the second floor of the restaurant.

'The Japanese are a curious people,' he told her over their dinner. 'Everything is different here.'

'Oh, is it so? How different?'

'Why, in many ways.' He lifted his brows momentarily, as if to take hold of the first thought which might come to him, 'Architecture, for example. You know: houses, buildings. A Japanese house is much different from an American house. The American house is built strong and its appearance is very important. The Japanese house seems to be built to,' he bit at his lip, not knowing how to express it, 'to be alive.'

Saeko laughed at him. 'No, I know no houses which are alive. I think you have a funny house.'

'Or take the men in buses, in trains, you know? Sometimes they stand up for children whereas, in America, children are often expected to stand up for their elders. For big people, you know.'

'Is it true? Which do you think is better? In America, a man stands up for the girl to sit down. Isn't it true?'

'Some gentlemen do, yes,' smiled Ephraim. 'Or,' he began again in a moment, averting his eyes, 'take this difference, take you for instance. You are a B-girl, that's what we call it.'

'B-girl? What is this?'

'Well,' he toyed with his fork, sorry he had brought it up but too curious to end it, 'in America, it is a bad thing to drink with strangers at a bar in the way you do; I mean, to order water and then ask the stranger to pay much money. This is called B-girl—bar girl, you understand? And a B-girl in America—well, I don't know, but she wouldn't be like you. For example . . . going to the shrine for my son . . . of course,' he chuckled awkwardly, 'there are no shrines in America, but . . . or coming to dinner with me now. Like this.'

'She would not have dinner with you?'

'Oh well, she might. But she would be pretty suspicious of me for asking her. But you just come along as if we're old friends. You don't distrust me, I think.'

She appeared to be at a loss, but since Ephraim didn't add anything to what he said, she lowered her eyes and told him, 'Soon, though, I am not B-girl. I am just maid soon. I think it is better.'

'Well, that's another switch,' Ephraim smiled. 'From B-girl to maid. Why are you doing that?'

'Because there is someone,' Saeko told him, 'who does not like me this way, I think.'

'Oh?' Ephraim felt his heart beating loudly, angrily, and tried to keep the inexplicable upheaval from his face. 'That young man?'

'No,' Saeko said. 'Not young man. Only me.'

Ephraim laughed more than was necessary. 'How old are you, Saeko?'

'Oh,' she laughed at his laughter, it seemed, 'I am twenty now.'

'Yes? Twenty?'

'How old are you?' she asked.

'Well,' his laughter fell away, 'old enough to be your father, really. I'm forty.'

'Then you live two years for each one I live. So you must know at least two times as much as I know. Isn't it so?'

'Look, will you tell me something else? Who was that young man? Was he your lover?'

'Young man . . . ah, Yoshio, Yoshio, yes? Oh, Yoshio is my good friend. But he does not love me.'

'Is that why you're becoming a maid?' he asked with a tight smile.

'I don't know,' she answered in her simple manner. 'One time, I say to myself all the things I want . . . but I cannot have such things . . . and so I think, there must be a way. But now I say to myself, I cannot have these things anyhow, and I think I may have nothing. So I decide to become maid. I have no talent.'

After dinner they walked, and after walking they went to a film. Saeko was more accessible than Ephraim had thought, and spent the night with him.

It wasn't until the next morning, when he had returned to the office in Yurakucho, that Ephraim received the telephone message from the house in Akiya which told him of his daughter's sickness. Unable to grasp anything more rational than fear from the message, he left Tokyo at once.

6

It seemed impossible that anything could come on the heels of Carl's death to drop him into still greater remorse, and he emptied his mind as the train carried him to Zushi. He was simply unwilling to place credence in the anxiety of the voice of his wife over the telephone.

Nancy had what a nearby Japanese doctor called 'a tiny touch of pneumonia', and since she was so small, every precaution should be taken. The doctor was a thin man with a narrow moustache and horn-rimmed glasses. Through an interpreter, he told Ephraim and his wife that if they were uncomfortable about his acting as the child's doctor, they might find an American doctor in the Military hospital at Yokosuka, or perhaps in Hayama.

Ephraim, wondering at the doctor's humility and afraid it might be a lack of confidence, decided to look for an American doctor at once. But his wife said softly to him, 'It doesn't matter, Ephraim.'

He looked at his wife in horror. 'What are you saying?'

'They won't spare her.'

'No?' Ephraim asked the neighbour who had come to interpret to try to reach the Yokosuka Naval Base. 'I'll tell you something, my dear. I'm worried

45

about you as well as Nancy, and when this is over, we're leaving Akiya. And leaving Japan, too.'

His wife walked away and Ephraim waited until he was given the telephone to talk to the administrative section at the American Naval Base Hospital. He described Nancy's condition and the doctor's uncertainty and asked to have an American medical officer sent at once. 'I'm sorry, Sir,' they told him, 'but it just doesn't sound like an emergency. We're sure your doctor can handle it, and we're guided by strict military regulations here. Even if it was an emergency, we couldn't send medical personnel out to civilians as far away as Akiya.'

'Well, I'll bring her in!' Ephraim shouted into the telephone.

'I'm sorry, Sir. If it sounded like a real emergency . . .'

'You mean if she had five minutes to live?'

'I'm sorry, Sir . . .'

Ephraim slammed the receiver down and went back to talk with the Japanese doctor, who was shocked to learn of the refusal of the Americans to help Ephraim. He at last suggested a Japanese hospital in Yokosuka, if Ephraim wished it; it was a very good hospital.

Ephraim, still unnerved by the doctor's previous want of confidence, decided to bring an American doctor down from Yokohama or Tokyo.

He was able to reach the office of a doctor in Tokyo who would come to Akiya the next evening, and who told Ephraim not to worry; from the description of it, Nancy wasn't too ill.

46

The Japanese doctor administered to the child that night and again the next day, and the American came in from Tokyo the evening of that day and examined her. The American's appearance beside the Japanese assuaged some of Ephraim's fear. The American doctor was tall, broad-shouldered and he exuded a kind of confidence even in his movements which was so positivistic that one had the feeling that if the American doctor couldn't help Nancy, then even God could not, nor could it be God's Will.

The following morning, Nancy died.

The Japanese doctor was called and he rushed to the house but it was too late. Ephraim telephoned the American doctor in Tokyo to tell him he needn't bother to bring his confidence back to Akiya, and the American comforted Ephraim with religious words. Ephraim thanked him and hung up and went back to the room where Nancy lay dead, and the Japanese doctor was slowly putting his things into his case. The doctor looked as uncertain about Nancy's death as he had been about her life. He didn't try to comfort Ephraim, but simply nodded his head and left the house.

It took Ephraim some days only to get into his grief. The shock was too complete, and coming upon Carl's death as it did, his ability to feel complete grief had a too recent obstacle before it. But when the awfulness of Nancy's death reached him at last, Ephraim nearly collapsed beneath it.

For two weeks, he didn't return to Tokyo.

He walked about Akiya, about Hayama, about

47

Zushi. He walked down to Hayashi one day and sat there watching the farming people run from one bus to another as they came in from Zushi or Yokosuka or Misaki. The people were shorter than his people, sad-eyed many of them, and yet nearly always cheerful. Even the oldest of them seemed energetic, deeply attached to living. He began to watch the children in particular. At first, they had seemed much alike to him, but now they seemed somehow more active, more engaged, than his own children had ever been. He wondered what the difference might have been between these children and his own, that these were surviving and his own had not, as though expecting that no foreign children could survive in Japan.

One day he ran into the Japanese doctor and stopped to talk with him, but the Japanese doctor spoke nearly no English. He only said, 'I am sorry,' and, 'Thank you,' to whatever Ephraim told him, and so they parted.

Another day, his neighbour who spoke English told him that the Japanese doctor was a very good doctor, and she didn't understand what Ephraim tried to tell her about the man's lack of confidence. She couldn't make a virtue out of the act of confidence itelf, and so Ephraim stopped speaking of it.

Then the woman, her eyes down, told Ephraim that the doctor had said: 'That child did not wish to live.'

Ephraim was startled at the idea and later thought about it. No one had been too worried about Nancy, and yet she had died. But, even admitting she had lost her only real playmate, and her brother, it seemed too horrible that she had simply stopped wanting to live, and Ephraim couldn't think of any reason why she would have lost the impulses of life.

7

Eventually he had to return to work.

It was good to get back to his desk, and the more so because his wife, who seemed distraught in no other way, had grown so phlegmatic in her companionship that she seldom answered Ephraim even if he spoke to her. She appeared just lazy. She was like something with a motor, and not a very good one. She did well enough without the maid, cooking and cleaning and even shopping, but she had nothing to say and was much to Ephraim as the maid had been.

Again, he took to working late, but again he took to visiting the bar in Shimbashi, to see Saeko and tell her of his new misfortune and find relaxation with her if with no one else. But she never seemed to appear at the little bar any more.

One day Ephraim spotted her friend, Yoshio, and asked if Yoshio remembered him. Yoshio did and Ephraim shook his hand lustily. 'Saeko-san,' Ephraim said, 'Doko . . . doko . . .'

'Ah, Saeko-san,' chuckled Yoshio. But what else he said was in Japanese and was no help to Ephraim.

Whether because of having seen the young man, or simply by chance, Saeko did return to the bar in Shimbashi one evening not long after, and Ephraim, who had not really expected to see her, felt himself become too warm with excitement and then too cold with surprise at his excitement. She saw him and came to sit beside him.

'Hello,' she announced happily. 'I have not seen you in so long time.'

'No,' he smiled, tapping his hand upon the bar, feeling guilty for the sensation of joy he felt at seeing the girl. He had told himself he wanted to see Saeko only to draw selfish comfort out of her, to speak to her of Nancy's death, but now he was afraid to speak of it, for fear of chasing her away. 'Where were you?'

'I? Oh, I work.'

'Of course. You're a maid.'

'I am maid in American house. Because I speak good English. So I don't come here much now, only to see friends sometime.'

'I still don't know why you became a maid.'

'Don't know?'

'I'll bet you don't make anywhere near as much money.'

Saeko shook her head. 'Maybe though,' she laughed, 'I am no good for being B-girl. Not so bad, really, you know? Easier than being maid. There is no one to take care of me and I don't live for other people's thoughts. Maybe I stop being B-girl, it is because you did not care for me that way.'

'Me?' He knew she was speaking lightly, and yet only hearing her say so made him feel peculiar, too happy. 'What have I got to do with it?'

'You say to me it may be bad, and I am thinking

51

anyhow there is nothing for me to get from such a life. So later I see you don't really care if I am bad or good, and so I am not happy. You ask me about Yoshio, if Yoshio will not marry me. Yoshio says he don't like old-fashioned girl. Some day, I think he marries old-fashioned girl. Anyhow, I am already thinking to stop being B-girl. Very hard, do you know? Now I am a maid. I have five-thousand yen each month. Very good, because in Japanese house, maybe only two-thousand five-hundred yen every month. I am only third maid.'

Ephraim watched the girl sip from the beer she had asked for and he tried to remember the conversation he had had with her. He hadn't meant her to think he hadn't cared whether she were 'good' or not, but had only wondered about the differences in her attitude and attitudes more familiar to him.

'Even so,' he finally said, 'five-thousand yen isn't much. For an American family in Japan.' He didn't like the idea that Saeko was a maid to Americans, even though he himself had had a maid. 'An American family can afford much more. I paid our maid fifteen-thousand yen.'

'First maid in this house, she get twenty thousand yen,' and later I get more too. It is not a bad job. Mrs Taylor is very kind to me, I don't have to do much. Sometimes take care of children.'

Ephraim ordered a second whisky.

'Some people say,' Saeko spoke after waiting for some while for Ephraim to say something, 'Americans come to Japan, pay big salary to maids, so maids maybe making more money than sometimes important people in big companies, you understand? Japanese people don't like this.'

'But you usually find it's pretty easy to hire maids at big salaries,' Ephraim said, a little sharply.

'It is hard to say no to good fortune,' Saeko smiled.

'Anyhow, it doesn't seem like much money to Americans, so what's the difference?'

His tone was still sharper, and Saeko eyed him unsurely for a few moments, then changed the subject: 'You are busy? I think you are always busy.'

'My daughter died,' Ephraim said suddenly, regretting it at once. He had felt defeated by her cheerfulness, by the wages of the first maid at Saeko's new house, by the lives of the children for whom she cared, even by what seemed a touch of contempt for the money he might have offered her; but then he felt ashamed of having brought up Nancy's death, particularly as he had: he was using his daughter's death to draw Saeko out of her cheerfulness.

Saeko didn't say anything and didn't look at him.

'Saeko,' Ephraim too kept his eyes on the bar, 'I keep thinking about you. I was looking for you for weeks.'

Saeko shook her head slowly. 'Is it true?'

'Saeko, I *did* care that you were . . . what you were doing . . . but now I care that you work for other Americans.'

She only continued to shake her head. 'Your little girl died?'

Neither spoke, and soon he saw that tears streamed down her face and he took her hand, but she snatched it free. 'No,' she said in a whisper through her tears. Then she said, 'I don't know what to tell to you. I am so sorry.'

'Listen,' he said quietly but also angrily, 'I want to tell you something. I am in love with you. I have known it for a long time.'

Again she shook her head. 'You are so unhappy. I am sorry. I am truly sorry. I cannot help you,' and she stood up. 'You are very unlucky. You are tragic and unlucky,' and then she hurried away, leaving Ephraim alone, as it had been after Carl's death.

He thought to go after her but had no energy for it, nor even much desire for it. She had been right, and he had been looking for an escape through her. He was unlucky; tragic! and he had wished her to share his tragic bad luck. Therefore, he thought, let her go; let her go back to her cheerfulness if she can regain it.

Ephraim asked for a third whisky and drank it quickly, reminding himself of his wife. Silent she might be, and odd in the eyes of any to see her these days, but she was still his wife and needed him more than before even if she didn't believe that was the case.

He had intended to remain the night in Tokyo, but instead went to Shimbashi Station and waited for the train to Zushi.

8

His wife seemed in somewhat better spirits that night. It wasn't that she had much to say, but only that her movements were sharper, and she might have been nearly ready to resign herself to the monstrous losses she had endured. Ephraim wanted to think that some of her improvement was due to the fact that he had returned home, and that night he tried to make love to his wife. She was permissive, and yet even as they sought to dart briefly out of truth, away from the house, his wife murmured: 'Ephraim, don't you wonder . . . who must be next? You or I?' Ephraim's interest died at once.

'We're moving,' he told her a little later, determined upon it. 'I've already spoken to agents in Tokyo. We'll take a small house in the city and I'll ask to be returned to America as soon as it can be arranged.' He had spoken to no agents, but he thought that the lie might lift his wife into an attitude of acquiescence.

'But Ephraim,' she told him, 'it doesn't matter if we move or not. It doesn't, really.'

'How about moving to Yokohama?'

'I know,' she said, her eyes closed. 'We'd be closer to the children. And yet, in a way, I feel as if we're closer right here.'

'Okay, we'll stay here until I arrange for being returned to America. I'm sure I can arrange it. God knows we've suffered enough here.'

But his wife laughed at that, and said, 'Do you think that would help?'

Ephraim resolved to make the arrangements without his wife's permission. It seemed to him he needed no permission from one under such queer delusions.

After a time, his wife said, 'Ephraim . . . it will be me. First, me.'

'What do you mean?' he muttered into the darkness.

'First, me. Ephraim, promise me we won't leave. Promise me you'll leave me with the children.'

He felt that he would weep if he tried to speak and he made no reply.

His wife's morbid certainty was such that he began to wonder about her fears, himself. After all, why had a seven-year-old Japanese boy been able to do so easily what Carl had not? The boy who had scaled the monster rock had been not only smaller than Carl, but a full year younger. And then, why had a touch of pneumonia taken Nancy's life? Why in God's name had his wife known Nancy would die when her illness had not been enough to quicken the action of doctors? And why did she have to persist in being, at Akiya, what she had never been elsewhere?

But the Whys of it remained unresolved and the ideas were too absurd to do anything but bring him wonder. His wife's excuse for everything seemed to be spirits, ghosts, a dreadful and inescapable fatalism. Ephraim listened to the night, to the wood and paper house, and heard the sea and many little sounds which might have been anything. He heard nothing to call spirits, to call ghosts, unless the ghosts were the sea and the night.

Finally he had the idea that Carl's death had brought his wife's mind into extraordinary contemplations upon death, and that in a sense—with Carl existing nowhere but in death—she had become devoted to death more deeply than she might ever have been devoted to life. With Nancy falling away from her, her devotion to death became that much more fascinating, and her certainty that she and Ephraim must also die was no more than a desire to be reunited with their children. Although, when he looked at it that way, Ephraim saw that there was as much hope and love in her morbidness as there was wretched darkness, still his wife seemed already more among the dead than the living. Beneath his covers, he shuddered.

Each day Ephraim attempted to gather the courage needed to talk out the necessity of returning to America with his wife. But each day the bare fact that his wife seemed to adapt herself to her gloomy life in Akiya, however remote from reality, sapped Ephraim of his courage. Her ability to depress him beyond toleration was too great, and her willingness too constant; she was, it occurred to him in a moment of grim humour, a sleeping dog, and he wasn't sure that he wished to disturb her, even in her own interest.

One evening his wife announced that she was feeling poorly and was going to bed if Ephraim wouldn't mind getting his own dinner. He tried to question the nature of her malady but she only smiled peculiarly and went to her room. Ephraim, while making his own dinner, couldn't escape the thought that his wife might actually mean to die, to leave him alone, and the thought frightened him.

The next morning she said, 'I don't feel like being up today. I wish you could bring someone in for a while.'

The words *for a while* annoyed Ephraim; it was as if it would be pointless to hire anyone with even tentative permanence because death was restless within the house. 'Look,' he said, 'won't you just tell me what the trouble is? I'd prefer calling a doctor if you really feel bad.'

'It's not bad,' she said all too mysteriously. 'But I think it would be better if there were someone here to do the cooking. I'm just a little weak.'

Ephraim grudgingly agreed and made a note to have his secretary call a domestic agency in Tokyo that afternoon.

All through the busy morning the confused worry about his wife intruded upon his work, and in the afternoon he finally forgot to worry in the surprise of receiving a Mr Inders at his office, a man he had known only from a distance in New York, who had now been sent to master whatever intricacies there were to Ephraim's job.

It seemed the main office, aware of Ephraim's double tragedy, had decided that he deserved a rest and would probably feel best about returning to America, and even though he hadn't applied for either the vacation or the change, Mr Inders had been sent to replace him. Ephraim was told that the company hoped he would be able to return to America within a month.

Ephraim tried to explain, without getting involved in spirits and the inexplicable, that his wife was ill herself, and that she was set against returning to America too precipitately. He said he wished the company had at least asked him for his opinion, and that in any event one month could prove too soon. He wondered what his wife would say when he told her of the company's decision; with luck, she might accede to a force beyond her husband's power, but without luck, she might be as resolved as ever to remain in Japan. One way or the other, his own ability to let the days drop behind him without bringing up the painful subject to his wife appeared to be at an end.

It wasn't until he had left the office that Ephraim remembered his need for a cook, and he wasn't sure whether he ought to eat out and worry about the cook the next day, or go home and be his own cook for another evening. Then he had an idea which, for no reason that he could grasp, terrified him. The girl Saeko might be the person to bring into the house.

He was magnetized by it the moment the idea struck him, thinking of what it might be like to have the pretty and sympathetic girl in the house at Akiya. He was willing to face no question other than the question of her willingness. But why not? She earned five-thousand yen with an American family in Tokyo. Why not fifteen, twenty-thousand, at Akiya? He felt some guilt at the idea but didn't question his guilt, and kept it at the back of his mind, and even as he contemplated the idea, he walked into Shimbashi. After all, he reminded himself, his wife wanted someone to be there, needed someone, and Saeko was the only girl he knew at all who actually might come on such immediate notice.

Finding her would be troublesome. The barman shook his head as Ephraim spoke slowly: 'Saeko-san . . . doko . . . Saeko-san no tokoro, ne? Doko . . .' The barman seemed to have understood, but his answer was beyond Ephraim's capability. Through gesture, Ephraim managed to have the barman write the address upon a piece of paper, and the barman did a bit better than that, appearing to have written the directions in the form of a sketchy little map.

But having given the paper to a taxi-driver, he found that the map took him to a house far across Tokyo, in Bunkyo-ku, a small house amongst other small houses, and surely too tiny to belong to the American family with three maids. He felt obliged to complete the investigation, however, and not finding a bell of any sort at the entrance, he stood back to call: 'Gomen kudasai . . . gomen kudasai . . .'

Soon a round-faced little boy appeared at the opened windows and grew wide-eyed to see Ephraim calling there. 'Saeko-san,' said Ephraim, hoping the boy would take some meaning from it and thinking this must be Saeko's own home. 'Saeko-san . . . *doko?*'

The boy shook his head and vanished. In his place there appeared none other than the young man Ephraim had seen with Saeko. Yoshio smiled in recognition and laughed heartily when Ephraim repeated his poor knowledge: 'Saeko-san . . . *doko?*' Ephraim felt sick and humiliated, certain the youth would think only one thing of Ephraim's anxiety, and indeed, what else could he think? Disliking the youth's laughter, Ephraim pinned his thoughts angrily to what he had begun, thinking, *Go through, Go through with it*, 'Saeko-san no uchi . . . *doko?*'

Yoshio shook his head, speaking Japanese. Probably, Ephraim decided, he was saying Saeko was at work and surely she couldn't be disturbed there. He glanced at his watch, wondering how long it would take to find the girl, and then he took the paper which the barman had given him and handed it to Yoshio along with his pen: 'Tokoro . . . *doko?*'

Yoshio understood. He gazed at Ephraim for a time, then suddenly laughed gaily. He put the paper up to a post and swiftly jotted down instructions. He handed the pen and paper back to Ephraim.

Ephraim studied the new map briefly and felt strange relief. '*Domo arigato*,' he all at once bowed low to the young man, and was surprised only by how naturally he was responding to Yoshio's helpfulness. '*Domo arigato gozaimashita!*' The young man, still grinning, made an uncertain half-bow to Ephraim and Ephraim swung about and hurried to the street.

It took a while to find another taxi, and this time the cab took him still farther back across Tokyo, into Meguro-ku. As they drove, Ephraim studied his map, wondered what he would say to Saeko, then wondered at the ease with which he had bowed to Yoshio. He had never before responded to either conversation or kindness except in the Western fashion, and it wasn't the bow itself which so much surprised him as that he had reacted without thinking about it. The taxi pulled up in darkness before a long stone fence, at the end of which there was a drive and gate. Ephraim motioned so that the driver would not go up the drive, then paid him and left the cab.

It was a quiet, twisting street, and once the taxi had gone, Ephraim felt more of the oddity of the situation. What impulse had led him there? No matter how mysterious the circumstances, what had made him decide to walk into a stranger's house and suggest that he hire a maid away from the people there? He stared at the high wrought-iron gate in dismay, thinking of the house in Akiya, remembering it in darkness, the beach, the sea, and again and again he thought of the too appealing melody of Toryanse. It was, if he would rid his mind of the spirit-like memories from Akiya, only a matter of going through the gate; the house of the Americans might have been a shrine, the gate a *torii*.

Not knowing what he would say, he went through the gate and up the gravel path to the porch of the Western-style house. There was a button there and he pressed it and directly inside a far-too-loud bell sounded. It seemed a long while before anyone answered, and then it was a fat Japanese lady dressed in the apron which identified her as a maid.

'Hello,' said Ephraim. 'I'd like to see the Master, please.'

'What?' she squinted through the darkness at him. 'What is it?'

'The Master of the house, is he at home?'

She kept squinting, then said, 'Minute, just a minute. Can't understand at all,' and she sounded annoyed, as if Ephraim ought to have spoken more clearly. Though he understood her, she had to run off after help, and in a few moments came back with a woman of about Ephraim's own age, an American with a sweet face which looked as if it had never frowned.

'Yes?' said the woman.

'I beg your pardon,' Ephraim began, nearly feeling himself about to bow again and restraining himself only as his muscles had initiated the act. 'This is a terrible intrusion. But you see,' he had to improvise, an unfamiliar art, and he used as many facts as he could, 'my wife is ill and we're in need of . . . of a maid, you see. You have here a girl . . . Saeko . . . Saeko-san. She . . . I know this is most rude of me, but I assure you there is no alternative.'

'I'm sorry, I don't understand. You're looking for

someone?' Without waiting for him to reply, she went on, 'Wouldn't you come in and have tea? Osen!'

'No no,' Ephraim lifted his hands, 'no. Please. If I could speak to the girl for just a few minutes. I'm sure she'll undertand.'

'What girl do you mean?' asked the woman.

'Why . . . Saeko-san. She is your third maid.'

'Saeko,' murmured the woman. 'You must mean the new maid? Osen! Please ask Horii-san to come out! Now, do I understand this girl has been your maid?'

'Well, you see,' Ephraim put his hands together, 'my wife is familiar with . . . she's become rather ill,' and then Saeko appeared and she seemed paralyzed as she caught sight of Ephraim.

Ephraim was himself at a loss and the words would no longer touch his tongue.

'This gentleman wished to see you,' said the American woman. 'Something about his wife being ill? I think you must know him, Horii-san?'

Saeko was more surprised than Ephraim had expected to hear that his wife was ill; perhaps it was the abrupt manner in which it was announced and, after what she knew already of his unbearable losses, she might have instantly presumed the worst. Saeko shook her head and, even as it had been when last he saw her, tears shot into her eyes: 'Your wife is sick? Oh, it is unlucky,' and he could see it was difficult for her not to simply let herself be free to cry.

Go through. 'Saeko-san,' he said. 'I have to speak

with you. May we?' He turned to the American woman, and she looked about as if thinking which room she might lend them, but Ephraim added, 'The porch will be fine. Please excuse me for being so rude.'

'Of course,' the American woman said. She smiled and gazed at Ephraim and Ephraim saw that her face, which seemed never to have frowned, looked equally disengaged from genuine cheerfulness, her smile seemed to have been pasted upon her pleasant features; he got the idea that she wasn't fooled at all, that she might not even have believed that his wife was ill, and that whether Saeko came home with him or not, she must surely lose her job in the house of this woman.

Then they were alone, the porch light left alight for them. Saeko mixed bewilderment, sorrow and surprise so artlessly in her face that Ephraim's guilt was renewed, and still more because her face was all at once wholly attractive to him. He was glad he had gone through.

'Saeko,' he said, then stopped and muttered, 'My God.' He looked down, then back to her. 'We need you.'

She couldn't do any more with her face than she had already done with it. She looked unable to know where to begin the search for an answer.

'I mean,' he looked around a little wildly, knowing he had to say something reasonable, 'my wife is ill. We need a maid.' More tears pressed from her eyes and Ephraim, thinking he was making matters worse, said, 'She isn't very ill, Saeko. It isn't a bad sickness.

65

But of course she feels we need . . . help. And I . . . I thought of you.' To him, it sounded weak, absurd.

'She is not badly sick?' Saeko at last asked.

'No no, not bad at all. But we need help, and,' how could he make such banal reasoning match the effort he had taken to find her? 'Saeko, please, for God's sake, please listen to me. I don't want to lie to you. Something made me come after you. Yes, truly, my wife needs help. But it is I who . . . once I thought of you, I couldn't think of anyone else. Please come to our house in Akiya.' Before she could say anything, he swiftly added, 'I certainly . . . I mean, I won't hurt you. If you think that.'

'Hurt me?' It only bewildered her further. 'You want me to work for you? Oh, but I have this job now. I am sorry. What do I do?'

'Listen. Saeko, listen. How about this? I'll pay you fifteen thousand yen. Or what salary would you like? All you have to do, really, is some cooking. You can cook?'

She gaped at him.

'Well,' he made himself chuckle, 'I'm sure you can cook. Otherwise, the whole thing is . . . well, what I mean is, will you come stay with us? For a while? I promise that if you decide to leave us, I'll find you another position, even better than the one you have here. Do you understand?'

She nodded slowly. 'You want me to be cook for you.'

'Well, will you?'

'But I am not good cook. It is true I am not.'

66

Against what he had done to get to her, it seemed a preposterous argument, and he said almost irritably, 'What does that matter?'

'But maybe it is bad if I leave this job. Not good for Mrs Taylor.'

'No no, don't be silly. She'll make out. She'll be all right, Saeko.'

'But your wife is sick?'

'Oh, it's nothing so bad. You needn't worry about her. I'm not asking you to be a nurse. I mean, we have a doctor nearby.'

She kept watching him.

'I want you to come with me,' he told her. 'To-night.'

'I cannot. I have work, even tonight.'

'I'll talk to Mrs Taylor myself.'

'Oh, she will be very angry.'

'What the hell right has she got to be angry with you? Anyhow, you'll be far away. We'll both be far away.'

Saeko waited, staring into his eyes as though hunting there for some meaning to all that had happened. 'Why do you ask me to come? Others are better than me.'

Ephraim didn't answer, but stared back at her and hoped his eyes would say what he himself hadn't the will to say, even to himself.

Saeko took him by surprise, then, saying, 'You think I am better than I am. Isn't it true?'

'What do you mean?' he asked, feeling his cheeks go hot.

'You say to yourself, I am so good, you must apologise to me, pretend to me.' She shook her head. 'Yet you know about me.'

'Know what?' he asked. She might have been trying to destroy his image of her, as if to make a negative answer to his plea, framed in the humility of truth.

'You are not like what I think, too, maybe. Sometimes you are more like teacher. Sometimes I go away from you, then I think about you, you know? I think how unhappy you are, because you are unlucky, but I like you. So it is not important that you pretend with me.'

'Saeko, I'm sorry. I don't understand you, and if I seem to pretend to you, it is only because I'm pretending to myself, as well. Sometimes pretence is best, even necessary.'

'So,' she said, as if she hadn't been listening, 'it is all right. I will go with you.'

Saeko went into the house and Ephraim, wondering at his victory, stood outside the porch taking his lungs full of the delicious night air. He had succeeded and now that he had got what he had come to get, the problems of getting it began to occur to him for the first time. It would seem strange to his wife that Saeko should come home with him, rather than—as a maid might be expected to do—merely put in an appearance the next day. Horii . . . Horii . . . he must remember her surname; it wouldn't help to be calling her in too friendly a manner at once. His awareness of self-deceit was so palpable that he had an attack of shame and regret. Well, perhaps it would be better to be

frank with his wife, to tell her he had forgotten to
have his secretary telephone the domestic agency,
had remembered the girl he had met who was a maid
—but that was stupid and even cruel, of course. He
began to think it might be wiser to take a night to
think it over, to ask Saeko to remain with the
Taylors another night, saying he would pick her up
after work the next evening. That was what he
should have done to begin with.

It was too late. She appeared at last—quite quickly
considering that she had had to resign her position
and get her things together into two small suitcases
in that short period. She was obviously ready to go
with him to Akiya, and it was no time to tell her
he was rethinking the matter and might wait a day.

'What did you tell her?' he asked as they walked
over the gravel, through the gate, into the street.
His voice was no longer excited, his manner no
longer nervous.

'I tell her, your wife is ill, I must go care for her.
She says to me, if third maid is still needed after-
wards, then I maybe come back here. She called the
taxi. We should wait here.'

Ephraim stood at the gate and mumbled, 'After-
wards.'

9

It was an uncomfortable ride into Zushi for Ephraim. He felt himself being too solicitous of Saeko, as though he was concealing something not only from himself but from her as well. Saeko seemed not to judge his solicitousness, and did her best to return his kindness in the form of concern for his wife, asking how she might best care for Mrs Rome. Ephraim said something about how she need not expect much trouble in that direction.

By the time they had reached Zushi, he seemed to have resigned himself to whatever he had done and the resignation cheered him. He was able to speak of the torture of the past weeks, and even alluded to the strangeness of his wife's attitude, although in the end he thought it best to let Saeko draw her own picture of his wife's queerness. He only said, 'Now she doesn't say much, Saeko, but before all this misery, she was quite different.'

'Oh,' Saeko said, 'of course this is so,' and the obviousness of her remark reminded Ephraim that, in fact, it wasn't strange that his wife was of a peculiar cast after the things which had happened.

Ephraim's wife was asleep when they arrived, and he somewhat clumsily showed Saeko her room, telling her she was surely tired and should sleep at once. Saeko, giving no awareness of his solicitous formality, bowed, said goodnight and slid the door shut.

The next morning his wife only smiled at the news that the new cook was already there. If she wondered about her arrival during the night, she kept her wondering as still as her remorse and even greeted Saeko more warmly than Ephraim could recall her ever having greeted their previous maid. Saeko went at once to the small kitchen to do what she could about making a Western-style breakfast. The breakfast was not well prepared and the coffee far too strong for Ephraim's wife, and yet she accepted it without complaint.

Ephraim left for work thinking more about his wife than about Saeko, not understanding his wife's easy satisfaction.

Curiously, he continued to work late. Without trying to explain it to himself, it seemed no less uncomfortable a situation at the house than it had been before Saeko arrived; perhaps even more so, and he came home only around midnight, seldom seeing Saeko.

One night, though, she was still up and made coffee for him. 'Do you too like such weak coffee?' she asked. 'I am ashamed to tell you I have made bad coffee until now. No one tells me, until I see she doesn't like it. She is so kind to me.'

'I prefer it strong,' he said, watching her move about the kitchen and unable to avoid comparing her to the woman his wife had been before Carl's death. The comparison was unfair to both women.

He knew his wife too well to be uncomfortable with her, her very way of moving was a part of his identity. On the other hand, and even though Saeko herself was at best attractive and not beautiful, his wife had never had the grace of Saeko's movements.

'Have some,' he said, noticing she brought only one cup to the table.

'Oh, no,' she smiled the same dim smile she always used at Akiya. 'I am only cook.'

'Have some,' he repeated.

'Then, all right.'

Ephraim asked Saeko how she was getting on with his wife. He hadn't imagined it would feel so strange to have the two in the house together, and was more interested in the question than his voice allowed. Saeko told him his wife was a very nice woman and that she seemed tired, mostly, and not really ill. She said that his wife was perhaps only sad.

Ephraim, the following morning, asked his wife the usual, 'How do you feel?' He had lost the bitter feeling he had felt at first when she answered, as usual, 'I think a little worse, Ephraim,' and then, when he had not suspected it at all, she all at once asked: 'Who is that girl?'

'Girl? You mean Saeko?'

'She's very kind, more like a friend than a cook. How long have you known her?'

Ephraim buttoned his shirt slowly. 'I met her just after Carl's death.'

His wife ought to have become angry, or at least her sadness should have deepened, but she only appeared to be thoughtful for a minute before repeating, 'I'm feeling just a little worse this morning. Ephraim, how have you been feeling?'

'Me?' He was angry. 'There's nothing wrong with me. If you're really feeling worse, I'm going to have Saeko fetch the doctor. I think you're just weak from staying in bed so much, but I'd rather be safe.'

'You're right, Ephraim. I don't need a doctor.'

'All the same, I'd rather have him look at you.'

'No, please don't. I don't need a doctor.'

But Ephraim left word with Sakeo to have the doctor called during the day, as much to have the doctor once again face his wife with the fact that there was nothing wrong with her as to reassure himself about it.

He returned to the house earlier that night, arriving before ten. Again, Saeko was up and Ephraim asked her what the doctor had said. She told him that the doctor was able to find nothing wrong with Mrs Rome, but agreed that she was tired and far from relieved of the shock of the tragedies which had so recently beset her, and it was perfectly natural that she should wish to do nothing but rest. She should rest, the doctor had said, so long as she wished to, and her own body and mind would provide her with the best prescriptions.

Somehow, Mrs Rome's malady seemed worse than that. It wasn't that she seemed more than tired, only that she seemed too tired. She left her room less and less, being awake didn't matter, and Saeko gradually accepted the household duties and attended to Ephraim's wife as well. Ephraim became accustomed to seeing Saeko more than his wife, and finally to eating with Saeko in the morning and, as he began coming back earlier, at night. It seemed pointless to spend too much time with his wife, for she had no wish to speak with him, nothing to say to him, and he could sit with her only so long examining her inertia.

10

Ephraim had put off his employers about returning to America, telling them his wife was in need of a complete and lengthy rest and was not up to such a laborious undertaking as a move across the Pacific and the breadth of the United States. He worried about the reaction of the people in New York to this, and the effects it would have upon his career, and yet he put them off so naturally that it seemed even to him there was more than his wife involved. After all, he had been with the company for more than a decade; he might have explained his wife's severe shock, suggested that plans be made for a swift and easy journey, and they would have been both sympathetic and helpful. Instead, he put them off almost coldly, leaving them no room for helpfulness. It was as though he were taking the action not to benefit his wife so much as himself. To their questions about when he might expect his wife to be sufficiently improved to travel, Ephraim replied vaguely. It was fairly impossible to say certainly, he wrote them, but he was thoroughly able to work, and hoped he might remain at his Tokyo desk so long as necessary.

The trouble with that was Mr Inders, who had quickly come to understand Ephraim's responsibilities and who had taken many of them upon his shoulders already. It became more and more difficult for Ephraim to work a full day, much less work late, and there were even days when it was ridiculous to go into Tokyo at all.

The doctor visited his wife twice each week, but only to allay Ephraim's concern, apparently, for he continued unable to find anything wrong with Mrs Rome. There was not even cause for occasional sedation, nor for the mildest medication; she was able to sleep and did not allow whatever shock she was feeling to reach the surface of her personality, or to affect her physically apart from her lethargy. Once Ephraim asked the doctor about the possibility of his wife needing psychiatric assistance. The doctor pinched at his small moustache thoughtfully and asked if Mrs Rome was religious.

'Not very much,' said Ephraim, but in a few moments he added: 'She's become superstitious, though,' and he spoke about the awe in which his wife had held strange notions about the Akiya house even before Carl's death, and the certainty she appeared to have had about it after his fall. She had seen Nancy's death as inevitable, and she now seemed to Ephraim to think that not only she, but even her husband, was doomed. The doctor was astonished and couldn't think what to suggest; he assured Ephraim it was baseless for his wife to have bad feelings about the house, that the story of the young man and woman was less than romantic, and that even if it had been romantic, there was nothing even in Japanese tradition to support any

76

qualms about ghosts of couples taking their lives together. But if the woman would understand that in every country there are people who choose to die when faced with too stern financial demands by life, then, the doctor said, she might realize the uselessness of seeking substance from the shadows.

'Tell me,' Ephraim asked, 'hadn't the young man any friends, any family, to help him? Surely he didn't need so much money.'

'Ah,' the doctor answered through Saeko, 'you see, the young man was Korean. His wife was Japanese. In this country, he had no family, and her family was not prepared to help the daughter who married a Korean against their wishes. Being a Korean, and having done some fishing at the till, he could fear not only punishment but even banishment upon discovery of his crime. The situation was bad, they saw no solution, and thus they took a terrible road out of it,' such was what Ephraim gathered the doctor tried to say; he concluded:

'But of course, now this has truly become a house of tragedy. There seems no need to think your wife needs psychiatric assistance because she is overcome by what would overcome any human being,' Ephraim looked away as he put the message together from Saeko's translation, 'Now, I had only wondered if spiritual assistance might be of help. But if she is not religious, perhaps there is no use in it.'

Usually, when the doctor visited, Ephraim didn't speak to him beyond a casual, 'Hello,' and it became more habit than concern to see the man with his

77

little case come walking through the house a few times each week.

At some weekends American friends from Tokyo visited Ephraim, to see and encourage him and visit and comfort his wife. It had been a strange experience, Ephraim knew, for these friends to see his wife as she was. She smiled at them as if from across the distance of her experiences, spoke softly without animation, often kept her eyes closed even as they spoke to her, often said nothing. And only when he saw his wife beside other American women did he understand how curious was her illness; she was an entirely different woman, and his friends—while sympathizing with Ephraim—obviously did not know what to make of her.

What seemed still more curious was that he himself did not have much to say to his friends. When they would leave his wife's room and perhaps sit over coffee at the table behind the house, the conversation would be too loose, would never take root in a subject or adopt a definite direction. He did not know whether he had himself changed in some way so that he no longer shared their interest, or whether they were aloof from embarrassment, but it was as if he had caught some of the morose germs which infected his wife, and he knew the Americans were as ill at ease with him as they had been with his wife.

Ephraim was going into Tokyo only two days each week, and some mornings he was able to induce his wife to walk with him along the sea-front, on warm mornings when the sea broke in whispers.

Such Autumn mornings were delicious and, walking with his wife in gloom and perplexion, Ephraim could still feel the thrill of the chill-touched cast of the morning sunlight, the clear sweet air from the sea, the smell of life and all that lives, and he felt how exciting it would be to walk there on such Autumn mornings in more pleasant circumstances. Helplessly, he thought of Saeko.

Sometimes children ran along the beach and he was afraid they made his wife reflect and he almost didn't like looking at the playing children, as if by not looking at them he might show his wife that they were not important enough to draw one's attention. But he did look at the children askance, sometimes remembering Carl and Nancy and growing sadder himself; and yet, at other times he saw them as life and beauty and the most natural part of the mornings. If he saw a boy who was small and about seven years, he would wonder if it might be the boy who skilfully mounted the rock which Carl had been unable to conquer, but he never looked at such a boy with dislike or envy, only with wonder. It was as if even that boy was merely a part of the whole new atmosphere which he had once thought he was ingesting, but which was in fact ingesting him, with all he had.

The very fact that she had taken to living in bed was making his wife weaker, and it became more and more of a struggle to try to rouse her from her bed for even a brief while. She would always say, with increasing legitimacy, 'I'm feeling too weak, Ephraim. Too weak.'

79

He frequently walked alone. While he enjoyed the beauty and richness of the Akiya mornings more by himself than with his wife, he didn't like being alone so much as he was, and wished he might now and again ask Saeko to walk with him. But he feared it would seem too odd to others that he should walk with his maid while his wife lay ill. Some mornings, when he was up very early, he induced Saeko to take short strolls with him, and convinced himself that she as well as he felt renewed by those mornings: the green and blue waters of Sagami could seem still more serene and gentle in their movement, taking on still more vivid colours from the shifting silvery vibrancy of the first sunlight of day, mixing violets, yellows, even touches of vermilion and pink, and far off, across the sea, Fuji appeared, peered momentarily, hovered, disintegrated, vanished. Nor did they have to speak as they walked, for the morning gave them its wealth and they received it together; it seemed enough to Ephraim that he was not alone, and that he knew the girl beside him, and that she knew him.

He became Saeko's lover one night, and so easily that it seemed they had been lovers all along. He had known her once before, and yet that was scarcely in his memory, it might have been another girl. The Saeko he knew now was met for the first time and for the hundredth time, and she accepted him still more generously and more dearly than he could remember having been accepted by his wife.

The night began to fall still more sweetly and freshly than the morning rose, or came to seem more like the sweetest mornings when the sun lifted and sent shimmering arrows of light across the sea, whose waters accepted the light gracefully and grew warm beneath it. It was too easy to linger in Saeko's room, and difficult to leave it, not for any passion which might have kept him there, but for the simple quiet warmth of what they shared, which brought him a kind of solace that, before Saeko, he had neither needed nor known. What made the moments seemed relived was that she gave expecting, and with animal grace and without the passion which besets the unaccustomed lover; and yet those were the very things which made the night into morning, which gave him the sense of meeting Saeko for the first time.

It became habitual to rise early, so that they might steal the dawn together by the seashore, as if needing some part of the daylight to share openly, a ritual of giving themselves to the purity of being seen, of not hiding. They never spoke much, for there was not a great lot about which to talk, and what there was to talk about was not altogether encouraging.

But Ephraim did try to tell Saeko that he was in love with her, at first with self-distrust, not certain that he wasn't using the word apologetically, but then using the word repeatedly and with assurance, even though he knew he was giving the word a new meaning. He wasn't sure what he felt for Saeko, and when he was by himself—on the train, walking in Tokyo or only sitting upon the beach—he attempted to put the new definition into words which he might explain to her, or at least to himself. What he felt was not the romantic love of a boy for a girl, or even

81

of a man for a woman; it was not what one expected to feel about a girl for whom one professed love, it could not belong in a film story. It was only a deep satisfaction with Saeko which was so whole as to provide a quiet excitement; and though the description seemed so dry as to sound nearly like rationalization, he could not think how to alter it. Saeko had come to please his eyes, her voice to please his ears, her manners to please his senses; her presence did not intensify his emotions, but rather relieved them of intensity.

There was something in the new relationship which made him blame himself for a kind of callousness, and he still recalled the words of the Japanese doctor, who had said he would express surprise only if one was not overcome, as his wife was, by the tragedies which had ruined his small family. He believed he would have been more moral to collapse, he would seem more virtuous if he, too, suffered from such shock that he would be unable to rise from it. But the virtue was beyond him, and although the guilt plagued him, still the vice persisted: and when Saeko entered a room, or if he only saw her from the beach or down the road, such wretched thoughts were dissipated at once.

The more satisfied he grew with Saeko's companionship, the more worried he became that his wife would see into the satisfaction and condemn it, and even though he suspected she was all too aware of the feeling he had for Saeko, he still went out of his way not to visit his wife at the same time that Saeko was in the room with her.

For a time, it was easy to adjust himself to all that he shared with Saeko, as if aided by the sheer relief it brought him. Saeko herself seemed to need no period of adjustment; rather, she had understood even when he brought her to Akiya that she was entering a new phase of her life, with the capacity of any phase to please or disappoint, and the very fact that she came was her assent to the properties of the new phase. Thinking of her in that way, Ephraim would again have the song *Toryanse* cross his mind: Go through, Go through . . . enter each phase of life with assent. Assent to life. If anything, it was too easy to adjust himself to the harmony of Saeko and the sea, Saeko and the house, and he began to understand how he could take out of the very concept of assent a kind of peace which comforted him even upon the deaths of his children.

One night he asked Saeko, 'Do you think you'll ever speak the word *love* to me?'

'Love?' she whispered, sounding oddly bewildered by the question.

'Would you be willing to live your life with me?' It was impossible to give his question a situation which had meaning.

'But I am living with you now.'

'But what if it could be always? Would you think you would want to?'

'There is your wife,' she said in a moment.

'I know, Saeko, but I mean if I had met you . . . if I didn't have a wife . . . and if I asked you to live with me, just like this, but always. Would you have wanted to?'

83

She seemed to have to chase his meanings down, but then said softly, 'I think so.'

He was satisfied with her answer and asked her no more.

Their life together, his wife to one side of them and his work to the other, was acceptable, but the time came, as he knew it must, when Ephraim was met with something like an ultimatum from New York. They pointed out that they could not continue to pay two men in Tokyo, and they were more certain of Inders than of Ephraim. Surely, they wrote, it would be better for his wife to rest in America; the plain invigoration of being among her own people, in her own environment, would do more for her than all the medicine in Japan. Ephraim couldn't think what to do to delay them, and he at length wrote back that his wife was for the moment worse rather than better, but that he hoped she would be able to travel in a month or so, and he would do all he could to ensure the earliest return possible. He also suggested that his wife was not suffering from any sickness which being in Japan, itself, could worsen, and that the company should feel free to continue its confidence in him if they chose to keep him there. He was capable of resuming the full measure of his responsibilities if they decided to send Inders back to New York. Inders himself was sympathetic towards Ephraim's situation, and was prepared to go to New York if the executive should decide that way, and Ephraim mentioned Inders' co-operative sympathy in his letter.

84

It was a poor letter at best, Ephraim decided as he left the office.

What if they should write back to him that they were willing to wait the month, even two months? Then in one or two months, he must be ready to pack his things, strengthen his wife to the task and leave Akiya, Saeko and crawl back into all the elements of his former life exclusive of the joy which had come from the children. He did not want to leave Akiya or Saeko, and could find nothing to recall of his former life which made him anxious to return to New York; there would be only more reminders there of the missing children, and no kind of harmony and no kind of love for compensation.

He began to visit the American Club, seeing some of his old acquaintances there, hoping he might catch on to the possibility of a position with one firm or another. It did no good, for it seemed that he himself was not the same individual he had been before he moved to Akiya. Once, leaving a friend at the bar in the basement of the Club, he even bowed, and then bowed again when the friend failed to respond, and only then did he realize that the men in the tiny stag bar were gaping at him, and that he was embarrassing his friend. They would not accept him because, he felt, he was held to be different, odd, either too quick to pick up Japanese ways or too dumbfounded yet by his afflictions. He was certain that he would find no help in the American Club, and once he stopped visiting the building he seemed to lose contact with all the Americans he had known.

11

He went into Tokyo only one day in the following week, but the one day was startling. Waiting for him in the offices he now shared with Inders was his brother, Aaron. Aaron Rome was a realtor in Seattle, and Ephraim had not seen him for many years. He had to look twice to be certain it was Aaron, and then he hugged Aaron and they sat and talked about banalities for some time, as if collecting the banalities to use them as a foundation to support the more sombre topics they had to discuss.

It was not until Ephraim had taken Aaron to lunch with him that he was told why Aaron had come to Tokyo.

'It was a free ride, Ephraim,' smiled Aaron. 'I couldn't turn it down.'

'I wondered if it was like that,' Ephraim nodded. 'Well, Frank Buck, I'm flattered of course. They actually paid your way here to see if you couldn't bring us back? That's very kind of them.'

'They are kind, Ephraim,' Aaron grew serious. 'They're trying to help you but they don't understand what the hell has come over you.'

'I thought I made it clear enough that it isn't what has come over me, but what has come over my wife.'

'Well, Ephraim, they've investigated that.'

'Investigated? What are you talking about?'

'They've been in touch with some Japanese doctor living down your way. He wasn't able to say much to them, but apparently the trouble is more shock than anything else and he didn't rule out travel.'

'How did they get his name?' Ephraim demanded angrily. 'And what right had they to pry like that behind my back?'

'They had that right,' Aaron said in a mild voice which displeased Ephraim since it too obviously tried to soothe him, 'because they know that you, yourself, have been shocked. Ephraim, they aren't spending money out of curiosity. They want to help you. They're trying to be decent to you, and I think they've been damned fine, if you want my opinion. After all, they might have dropped you before this. And if they did, you'd both be forced to leave the country, I suppose.'

'Well, that's not true, Aaron, that's not true at all. My visa doesn't stipulate that I work for any specific organization. Nor are they the best paying office over here, even in my field.'

'Come on, Ephraim,' Aaron still tried to soothe him, his words as soft and playful as if he were trying to ease a child's bad temper, 'you know as well as I do that there's no one to give you a position over here. They investigated that.'

'Investigated that? Well, they just investigated a hell of a lot, didn't they?' snapped Ephraim. 'And I wonder if they didn't really arrange that. It's quite interesting, Aaron, quite interesting.'

'All of which took them time and money,' Aaron

reminded him gently, smiling. 'They're offering, it seems to me, every—'

'I *wish* you wouldn't take that sweet tone, Aaron, *please* don't! You sound like a phony analyst trying to calm a maniac, and I wish you'd just talk. I don't need petting.'

Aaron's cheeks reddened and he ate for awhile without speaking. Then he said somewhat stiffly, 'But it's true. They've done a lot for you. I think it's your due to both appreciate and respect what they've done.'

'Did they get my letter?'

'They told me about one letter they received just before I came. You asked for a month or so? Was that the one?'

'And may I ask what was their reaction?'

'The same as it's been all along. They want to help, and if you'll be a little more definite with them, they'll go along with you as far as Christian reason can allow. Ephraim, I don't know how to handle this, I admit it. I've told you how terrible we all felt to learn of what happened, and maybe by now I would have killed myself, in your place. How you've stood up under it at all is beyond me.'

'Well for Christ's sake,' Ephraim was angrier than his brother had expected at those words, 'I *am* a man, you know. I *am* alive!'

Aaron blinked, then went on, 'But the fact remains, it's all past now, and all they or I or anyone can do is try to help you take the pieces that are left and put them into some reasonable shape together, for the future. You're young yet, you're both young yet. You've both got to start again, don't you see? I want you to come back with me. Right away.'

'When?'

'In a few days. A week at the most, but try to make it less, Ephraim, please. I'm not helping my own business by being away right now.'

'It's out of the question.'

'All right. A week then.'

'It's out of the question.'

'Oh, don't be stubborn. However much you've suffered, Ephraim, don't be stubborn. Just wake up for long enough to get out of this country, and take my word for it that it's going to be the best stimulus for both of you. Do this for me, Ephraim, for all of us.'

'Even if I agreed to it,' Ephraim scowled, 'do you think *she* would?'

'She'll have to.'

'I won't remove her by force. It would destroy her. If there's one thing I'm sure of, it's that.'

'Ephraim, isn't it because she doesn't wish to leave the children behind? Isn't that it?'

'That's part of it,' Ephraim admitted grudgingly. 'There's more.'

'But they're willing to pay the costs of reinterment in the States. Now, I tell you, there aren't many employers who would do for anyone what yours are doing for you. In a way they may feel responsible. They sent you here. Try to return their responsibility to you in kind. Don't disappoint them. Remember, you owe them plenty.'

Ephraim shook his head and scoffed, 'Reinterment! Do you really think Saeko would permit that?'

'Saeko?'

'I mean . . . you know what I mean . . . she wouldn't hear of it!' Ephraim was all at once amazed and involved in an intense struggle to remember his wife's name. He couldn't grasp it.

Aaron insisted that Ephraim was setting up one artificial obstacle after another, and all it proved was that he, himself, was in too bad a state to make an important decision just now. He begged Ephraim to leave it to his brother to make the immediate decisions and all the necessary arrangements, and simply to follow along until they were all back in America. Then Ephraim could rest as long as necessary, and so could his wife. Ephraim, angry and confused, said he would consider it, and suddenly he wanted to be away from his brother.

'You can get back to your hotel, can't you? It's very near. I'll meet you at Zushi Station tomorrow. Twelve fifteen.' He stood up.

'Think over all I've said, Ephraim,' his brother looked up at him with sad eyes. 'Just think over all I've said.'

'Yes,' Ephraim nodded, and then he bowed before his brother. 'Thank you,' he said with unconscious formality.

His brother only stared at him.

Ephraim, instead of returning to the office, walked about for a time. He walked slowly, looking at the quick movements of Tokyo all about him. He began to study the people who passed him, who stood about, who window-shopped and chatted and waited for trams and buses, and he tried to observe the differences between himself and each of them: physical differences, differences in gesture, differences in the life written into their faces. But the more he sought to locate and examine the differences, the less he was able to see them at all.

He took a taxi to Tokyo Station and, going through Yaesuguchi, climbed the stairs to the thirteenth line and watched the people waiting there for the Yokosuka and Shonan trains. Among them were American marines, youths with pink lips, tanned cheeks and blue eyes, tall and lanky, and they looked far from relaxed, too self-conscious, as they stood in crowds of Japanese. There were two elderly American women whose mouths were drawn down severely, who looked angry.

His train came and Ephraim got into a First Class coach and sat across the aisle from the two American women, who dropped into clipped and muted conversation on topics ranging from their church to Japanese food, and then the train jerked and pulled slowly out of the station and Ephraim couldn't make out their words.

The American women left the train at Yokohama, one of them smiling barely at Ephraim as she got up from her soft blue train-chair. Ephraim blinked and smiled back, inclining his head. It seemed strange to him that the woman had smiled at him but then thought she had smiled to him as an American to an

American in an outpost far from America, and he realized that he had been studying the Americans as though he was foreign to them. 'Good God,' he told himself, 'it's not the Japanese who are different, it's them . . . *them,*' they seemed all at once totally different from him, they would be ridiculous appendages to the house at Akiya, they could not move through its rooms or through its doors as did Saeko, they would not even be able to speak to Saeko without some awareness of difference between themselves and her, they could not stand upon the Akiya beach without looking transplanted. It was fantastic, but he accepted the fantastic truth: Americans were different from himself.

Aboard the bus that afternoon were three American girls, young wives of American Military personnel in the Kanagawa area, many of whom lived in or about Hayama. One of them was attractive and she noticed Ephraim studying her and looked away. The other two girls were chatting together, and the attractive girl sat alone. All three of them, even the attractive one, seemed somehow ill at ease, seemed nearly to be preening, and Ephraim wondered why. The conductress passed through the bus, selling her tiny paper tickets, and Ephraim noticed that the American girls looked down as they bought their tickets, as if somehow embarrassed to meet the eyes of the conductress directly. What could explain their embarrassment? Did they feel put upon, feel their foreignness too exaggeratedly? Was it that, being Military wives, they were cowed by the unpopularity of the American Military in Japan? He wondered if they felt either superiority or inferiority; certainly they seemed to feel difference.

The conductress herself was not a bad-looking girl, but not lovely in any way, and Ephraim looked at her more closely. She wore a black uniform jacket and black trousers which hung baggily from her hips and legs, a bad fit; her leather bag swung down from its long strap and her short fingers reached into the bag and inserted coins and snatched coins, and her face remained impassive, expressionless. When she came to him, Ephraim gave her a hundred yen note and looked intensely into her face. Her eyes looked down and they seemed nearly closed as she tore off and punched his ticket, and Ephraim saw that he had been wrong: she was lovely, lovely even as the face of a Kwannon was lovely. There was something in her face, vacant as she kept it, which was soft and confident, and perhaps this was the source of the embarrassment suffered by the young Americans, that they knew that this plain Japanese girl was, for something beyond her appearance and beyond their assimilation, lovely, through which she represented a kind of competition to which they could only remain aloof.

When he arrived at the house, his wife was reading from the book of classical Japanese poems he had purchased long before, and she set the book down to smile wearily at Ephraim. 'Oh, these are beautiful poems,' she told him in a languorous voice, unlike her. Lately, Ephraim couldn't tell what his wife was thinking or feeling because her outward aspects had become so altered. The habits of character she had once used and by which he judged her personality, she no longer employed, and seemed to have forgotten. 'Ephraim, when did you buy this book?'

'Don't you remember?' he asked absently. 'It was just after we moved here. I was picking things up to read on the train. Never read much, I'm afraid. I still have about five books at the office.'

'They're nice poems. There is one I like especially by Hitomaro, that's his name. Did you read it? He was a man who loved his wife very much.'

'Yes, I remember it,' Ephraim told her. He sat down and gazed at his wife. How strange the woman had become. He thought of his brother confronting her and wondered what each would think. He wasn't even sure his wife would remember his brother and asked, 'Do you remember Aaron?' It sounded silly.

'Your brother? Of course. Why?'

'He's in Japan. I saw him today.'

She let her eyes grow worried and said, 'Is he here to make us go back?'

'Well yes, I think that's his main purpose,' Ephraim said quietly.

'You know I won't go back,' she shook her head.

'We may have to. I can't hold on to my job over here much longer. I've got to tell you something. The company has offered to pay the costs of . . . of taking the children to America,' he looked into her empty face, then away again. 'Reinterment. Do you understand?'

'Ephraim.' She shook her head slowly. 'That's aw-

ful. I won't have them disturbed. No no, Ephraim,
we can't do that. Please tell your brother to leave us
alone.'

'He's coming down here tomorrow.'

'I don't want to see him if he's going to talk
about moving Carl and Nancy.'

'But I can't refuse to let him come.'

'Why can't they see that it doesn't matter now
and simply leave us alone?'

'You've got to see,' Ehpraim leaned back in the
chair, closing his eyes, 'that they can't understand
all of this. Neither can I, to tell the truth, and I
don't think you're doing a good job of it, yourself.
The company is being very decent. They could have
let me go long before this, but instead they've sent
Aaron over here—paid his way—and they've made
the offer to . . . about the children. They're only
trying to help.'

'You know they can't help us now,' she told him,
and as he opened his eyes, she closed hers. Still
again, he examined her face, as he had examined the
faces in Tokyo, on the train, on the bus. His wife's
face, though paler than it had once been and even
though it was possessed of a calm not really peculiar
to it, was drawn out severely, was not soft and what
confidence it bore was not the confidence of life but
only the confidence of determination. 'It really
doesn't matter if you keep your job or not, Ephraim.
I'm sure you must know that by now.'

Ephraim was not shocked. 'You think I must die,
don't you?'

95

'Well, Ephraim,' she kept her eyes closed, but then only said, as if trying to be clever through her desperation, 'everyone must die.'

'First you,' he said, 'and then me. And then they'll have their revenge, is that it?'

'I don't know if it's revenge, I really don't. Sometimes, as I lie here, I see it all as a series of events, like dominoes falling, and you can hardly call it revenge upon the last domino in the line just because the first has fallen. Sometimes it even seems that the sooner the last domino falls, the better. I know that must sound cruel, Ephraim. Especially if you don't understand about . . . the way it's happening. I don't mean to be cruel.'

'Listen,' he told her, abruptly angry and impatient, 'there isn't anything wrong with you. Nothing at all. And you know it.'

She only smiled again. 'I'm sorry, Ephraim. Please, I wish you'd leave me alone now. Just reading makes me tired, and I can't talk for long without wanting to sleep.'

'Well, you just get ready to snap out of this, you hear? You've got to start getting up at least a little bit each day. Do you hear?'

She didn't answer for a minute, then set the book of poems aside, holding her hand upon it. 'Yes, Ephraim, I remember . . . I wonder why I forgot . . . you bought that book just before Carl's death, didn't you?' She lay back, her eyes closed.

Ephraim arose, deeply irritated. He hadn't wanted to argue his brother's case to begin with, but the reaction of his wife seemed to him more than neurotic: it was vain and selfish. 'All right,' he told her, 'you die. If that's what you're set on, you lie there and rot, but I'm not going to fit myself into the insane plan you've drawn. You hear? You hear? I'm not going to die!'

He left the room and hurried out to the beach, to walk along the moving sea and rid himself of his angry energy in that way.

Over dinner, he told Saeko that his brother was coming the next day, with the sole purpose of trying to convince the Romes that they should return to America at once. He waited to see how Saeko would take the news, but she gave him no sign of her feelings. He next told Saeko of his wife's conviction that even he had to die, and Saeko tried to smile at it, but then said sadly, 'You do not have to die. I do not want that you die,' to which Ephraim retorted: 'I have no intention of dying!'

12

He took the bus into Zushi to meet Aaron, and brought his brother back to Akiya in a taxi, introducing him to Saeko and then taking him to his wife's room.

Aaron smiled at Ephraim's wife even as he had smiled at Ephraim the day before, with a condescension which seemed to Ephraim dreadful, but Mrs Rome didn't seem to notice. She let Aaron hold her hand and listened to him for so long as he wished to speak, and Ephraim was fascinated to see the degree of resignation she brought to bear against his brother. 'No,' she said softly, 'you don't understand. No, there's no point in our returning at this time. It wouldn't be for the best. No, I'm sorry Aaron, it wouldn't work out. Oh, I would feel too badly about moving the children, you must understand. Oh, Aaron, after seeing you take all this trouble for us, I'm so ashamed to appear stubborn, but it's best, it's best. No, no, I'm sorry, no.' Nothing Aaron said could move her and Ephraim was actually relieved when Aaron at last left the room and they walked out on to the beach together.

'Of course, she's got to be brought home,' Aaron told Ephraim. 'She's in a bad way, a bad way, Ephraim. Good God, do I have to tell you that?

How long are you going to let her lie there like that? You say she hasn't been out of that room for weeks? And you're doing nothing about it?'

Ephraim defended himself as best he could. He pointed out that the doctor came twice weekly, that the doctor's advice was to allow his wife's wishes to be her own prescriptions, but Aaron scoffed.

'She'll prescribe herself into such a profound state of mental agony she'll never emerge from it. Ephraim, for her own sake, she's got to be moved.'

Ephraim shook his head and pointed out that his wife was somewhat worse than she had been only a few weeks before, even suffering an occasional lapse of memory, and that he would have to wait for an answer to the letter he had sent asking for a delay of a good month at least. That would give his wife a chance to recover at least a little, and to prepare her for the return.

But Aaron said, 'She's worse today than she was a few weeks ago. And what if she's worse in a month than she is today?'

'Well, that's my decision, Aaron,' Ephraim replied firmly.

'You're killing her, Ephraim.'

Ephraim glared at his brother. 'How can you say that?'

'You're killing her.'

Ephraim watched Aaron through narrowed eyes for a few moments, then said, 'We'd better go on in. Saeko will have lunch ready.'

Aaron spent the entire afternoon and evening going over each detail of his case, and Ephraim did his best to rebut each detail, until Aaron finally said, 'Are you aware of how hard you're fighting me? Why? It's more than worry about her health, isn't it?'

'Don't be foolish,' Ephraim said tightly.

'You want to remain here? Why, for God's sake? Why?'

Ephraim thought about it and decided there was nothing he could say to his brother. All the things which motivated his desires were only sketchily explicable even to himself.

'Very well,' his brother sat back. 'What am I supposed to tell your employer?'

'I don't care what you tell him. You might tell him to stop arranging it for me to find it difficult to get other work in Tokyo, if you have to tell him anything.'

'Should I lie to him?'

'No no, of course not,' growled Ephraim. 'What are you? Your brother's keeper? Tell them something has happened to my eyes, to my nose, tell them I've shrunk a few inches and my hair has gone to pitch. Tell them I'm different.'

'What are you talking about?'

'Very well,' Ephraim went on, 'tell them I'm recalcitrant. I won't see reason. Tell them they'll have to discharge me instantly and forget about me. In fact, that may be the best thing all around.'

'You know I can't tell them that.'

'I don't give a good God-damn what you tell them, Aaron.'

100

'What is it, Ephraim? Tell me what it is. What's keeping you here?'

Ephraim continued to glare at his brother.

'Are you in any kind of trouble?' Aaron persisted. 'Is there a woman? That maid? Good God, she isn't even attractive!'

Ephraim didn't move.

'Well,' Aaron said sharply, 'I can't help you if you don't tell me what's at the root of it all.'

'I didn't ask you to help me.'

'But I've got to help you!'

'You could have helped me best by not coming.'

'That's an ugly thing to say.'

'I don't mean it as it sounded,' Ephraim tried to soften his glare, 'but you didn't come on your own, did you? It was a favour for the company.'

'Do you really believe that?' Aaron looked as if, at that moment, he surrendered his case. 'My God, you're as sick as she is if you think I came to help anyone but you.'

'You can't help me, Aaron.'

'Not if you aren't honest with me, no.'

'I've been as honest as I can,' Ephraim said vaguely.

'But why won't you tell me what it is that's keeping you here?'

'Because I don't know.'

'You must know!'

'I don't know,' Ephraim repeated, adding weakly, 'exactly.'

Ephraim refused to say anything more about it,

and Aaron asked if he could see him again the next day. He looked at Ephraim in disbelief when he said, 'It's probably better if you don't, Aaron.'

'You won't see me?'

'It's better if we don't try to fight it out. It won't do any good.'

'Then you simply refuse to return? And what am I to say? My brother is mad and his wife is mad and consequently they are beyond our help, so let's forget about them? What are you asking of me, Ephraim?'

'I ask nothing of you. I ask you to leave me alone for the time being. Call us mad, call us what you will, but forget about us for the time being. I have to work it out myself.'

Then there was a silence between them, and the conversation seemed to have put between them not only the stillness but a gap in understanding which, Ephraim felt, was so serious it might prove lasting.

'Well then,' Aaron finally got to his feet. 'I'm sorry, Ephraim. I swear to you I meant only to help you.'

'I know that,' Ephraim stood beside his brother. 'For that, I thank you.'

'I ought to have you both dragged back. I ought to report you both as lunatics and have you dragged back.'

'I'm sure you won't do that.'

'No, I won't.'

'Aaron . . . one more thing. I hate to ask this. But I'm terribly worried about my job.'

Aaron shrugged. 'I feel unclean about it, but I'll

do what I can. I'll tell them your wife is sicker than we thought. I'll ask them to respect your letter and be patient, if they will. Is there something else you want me to tell them?'

'Aaron, what I mean to ask . . . and I appreciate what you say, but we both know it won't do much good . . . but if you could let me borrow a thousand or so; just till things work themselves out.'

Aaron shook his head. 'I won't do it. I haven't the money, anyhow.'

'You know you could raise it.'

'I won't even try to, Ephraim. It isn't fair of you to ask me to contribute to your delirium. I want you to come back. If you'll promise to come back, I'll raise the money and pay your way myself. But I won't loan you a penny to continue this.'

Ephraim nodded.

He called Saeko and asked her to telephone for a taxi, and walked behind his brother as Aaron answered the cab driver's horn. 'I'll be at the hotel all day tomorrow,' Aaron looked out of the tiny car's opened window; 'Please change your mind and call me.'

Ephraim backed away from the taxi and bowed: 'Thank you . . . goodnight.'

The taxi pressed away into the darkness and the Akiya night with its quiet sweet sounds, the sea, a distant dog, the chatter of passing old men, instantly began to rekindle something like contentment in Ephraim.

Rather than go into the house at once, he decided to walk down the narrow highway a bit. He walked slowly, thinking of some of the things his brother had said, and when he passed a little vegetable store, the almost toothless lady who kept it turned to bow to him, grinning and calling: 'Komban wa . . .' Ephraim returned her bow, her 'Komban wa,' and even her grin. Only a minute later, a young boy on a bicycle nearly hit him and, recognizing Ephraim, said, 'Sorry,' even as Ephraim caught the bicycle and kept it from turning over; they both laughed and Ephraim told the boy to be careful in simple, stiff Japanese. The people of the neighbourhood had grown used to seeing him, and perhaps the tragedies he had suffered had hurried the process of their accepting him as a human being. He felt a serene attachment to the people of Akiya as he finally returned to the house.

Saeko asked him, 'Will you leave now?'

Ephraim shook his head.

13

He did not telephone his brother the next day, but Aaron called him the day after that in one last effort to convince Ephraim that he should leave Akiya. Ephraim refused to discuss it and his brother said that since that was the case, he would be leaving Japan at once; his own business would suffer if he remained away from it for long.

By the following week, things seemed to have settled back into the places they belonged, or at least had occupied before Aaron's intrusion upon them. The greatest worry Ephraim had was for the answer to the letter he had written, for he had still got no reply to it. His brother's visit had been one kind of answer, but obviously that visit had been planned before he had written his letter, and then Aaron had promised to confirm what Ephraim wrote. It wasn't hope for a single month which made Ephraim pay attention to the hour of the postman's visit, but hope that they would accept the delay graciously enough so that, on top of this hope, he could construct further hopes of retaining his position in Tokyo. A number of days passed, his moments alternating between anxiety for his position, deepening himself into the Akiya strata in which, somehow, his children lay buried, and caring for his wife as Saeko cared for him; and during each day he would pace within the house or at its front until the postman had stopped or passed on his bicycle, and the letter did not come.

'You know,' he told Saeko one night, 'I'm beginning to understand how my wife feels about this house. Do you understand? There's something here, whether the house or the beach or the people or whatever, which makes the children linger and seem —not alive, no—but, but more real. You see? I wonder why. One has the feeling that, if the children have spirits, those spirits would be here rather than in any other place. Well, I'm crazy too, don't you think so?'

Saeko smiled, saying nothing.

'Do you understand?' he asked.

She seemed to understand only partly. 'I think you miss your little boy and little girl.'

That was an odd answer, for Ephraim took that much for granted. Because what he said had made such a light effect upon Saeko, he rethought it and decided that it had very little to do with Akiya; it might have happened at Yokohama or Tokyo, or San Francisco or Hong Kong, and he would have adopted a special and incomprehensible and inescapable relationship to that place.

Sometimes, when he walked along the beach or down the road, he thought about his brother's visit and the frightening accusation his brother had flung at him: 'You're killing her,' and he could still grow incensed at the cruelty in the remark. He might as well have been accused of killing the children, or of inventing his wife's attachment to this place, much less his own. But however cruel it seemed, he could not dislodge the idea and sometimes he sat by his wife for hours at a stretch, telling himself that by being beside her he was in some way helping her. She did not speak to him, and only seldom looked at him, as he sat with her.

His wife appeared to enjoy nothing so much as lying back and thinking—just thinking—and, next to that, preferred reading, and only next to that did she seem to take any enjoyment from Ephraim's companionship. It certainly seemed that, if he was not killing her, he was at least allowing her to assume the rôle of death in life; but even for that he could not accept complete blame, for her attitude never changed and she was never willing to approach the possibility of leaving Akiya, even the possibility of spending a reasonable period of time out of her bed. He was bold enough to suggest that they leave the house more than once, and even borrowed some of his brother's cruel conviction in speaking to her: 'How long will you lie there, a self-appointed invalid, letting yourself be taken care of even to your toilet?' She looked at him too abjectly and he winced. 'Ephraim,' she said, 'you don't think I'm sick at all, do you?' 'No,' he replied, not looking at her, 'you're not sick. And your moral strength is somewhat less than I had believed, too.'

All of Ephraim's efforts to anger her out of her bed were as futile as simple pleading.

When he had nearly stopped expecting an answer to his letter, and nearly begun to hope that things might remain as they were indefinitely in so far as his work was concerned, the letter came. It was brief and to the point, telling him that he would be allowed a month from the receipt of the letter in which to plan, but at the end of the month he should either be prepared to return to America or make his own plans outside the organization. It was, if coolly stated, what Ephraim had asked for, but it was far too final. There was not a trace of patience in the letter, no remnants of whatever sympathy they might previously have felt. The letter seemed wholly useless. If he had received it two weeks before, then half of the month would be gone already. The month which lay before him seemed measurable in minutes.

Forgetting that the company had sent Aaron to Tokyo, had asked him to rest, had given him weeks already, Ephraim thought only of the decade and more of years he had spent with the company, and of the amount of time he had given them beyond eight hour days and forty hour weeks. He had been considered one of their best men, not so much because of any inspired talent but because he had always given the company all it could need and ask for on any job it had delegated to him, he had given it the labour of caring. He believed he looked forward to a career close to the top of the company in another fifteen years or so. Yet now, with a note as though addressed to a stranger, he was given a month.

He dutifully told Saeko about the letter, complaining to her about the company's brevity of loyalty.

Again she asked him, 'Will you leave now?'

He told her he would not leave, but that things could be difficult for a time. 'I'll have to find another job, Saeko.'

'But please don't say it is better that I leave. I will take care of your wife.'

He stared at her. 'Saeko, I certainly wasn't going to suggest that you leave. Good God, you're my reason.'

Saeko's smiles always seemed untelling to Ephraim, by themselves, but he had evolved a way of judging them by the moments in which they appeared, and he appreciated her immediate smile, and was even excited by it. 'Then I will not leave,' she told him.

Ephraim, trying to make sense out of the month he had in which to make sense, came upon the idea that his wife was in one way already dead. She lay in a kind of stupor, and nothing he said, nothing the doctor said, no threat of his employers, not even the visit of his brother, nothing could bring her out of it. His brother had been right about one thing: it might be helpful, however cruel, to have his wife sent back to America, even against her wishes. But even as he had the thought, he was aware that he was thinking of sending his wife to America without him; after all, it was not so unfair. He wasn't upon his back, as she was upon hers. He had been overwhelmed, yes, but still had his faculties, he had

109

not been conquered, and he still walked among the living; and while she lay beyond his help, he had sought to examine his feelings, had sought to understand his new attachments more rationally than she, and had even begun a new life in Akiya. It would have been a fresh life, at any rate, if his wife did not lie there, a lifeless but living tie to the ruins of his former life. The thought was pointless. He knew he would never be able to bring himself to the act of sending his wife back to America without him.

During the first weeks of the fearful, fast-moving month, the only minutes which seemed uncutting were those he spent with Saeko, beside her and with her in her small room. The room became the centre of Akiya, and the night stayed sweeter than daylight. Saeko seemed to him to have been born for understanding, perhaps because she had not been born into easiness herself, and knew sadness and trouble, and had even known the necessity for a kind of terrible surrender. Whatever it was, she could anticipate his thoughts, his moods, and her hands and voice and eyes shaded him from the heat of the furious world which appeared all too ready to destroy him.

He had again written to his brother, asking for the loan of a thousand dollars, even less, but his brother, writing quickly, refused. Aaron said he would send passage which could not be exchanged for cash, but beyond that he would feel worse about lending Ephraim assistance than denying him. Ephraim crumpled the letter, tossed it away and his brother left his thoughts.

Once more, he took to visiting the American Club, and he also visited a number of Western firms in Toyko and finally applied to Japanese concerns, although it meant applying for a drastically reduced wage. Being unable to speak more than a smattering of Japanese, he was unable to receive any offers except one which would pay him ten thousand yen each month for a few hours at the head of an English conversation class, less than enough to pay the salary he had offered Saeko.

He could not forget his anger with the company. He thought of writing to them once again and demanding another month, but he knew this would not be granted. It might be more likely, he thought, to apply for a loan of some sort against his salary when, with things settled once again, he could return to the company on any terms they chose. He mentioned that idea to Inders in Tokyo one day, but Inders screwed up his mouth and shook his head. 'I'm sorry, Rome,' Inders told him, 'they wouldn't do that. You can try, of course, but it wouldn't work. Look, if I had money myself, I'd do what I could for you. As it is, if you ever need a twenty, you know, or,' but Ephraim left before Inders could complete the meaningless, humiliating offer.

After visiting his wife and watching her fall from a sleepful awakeness into a pale sleep one night, he said to Saeko, 'Why don't we go into Tokyo for a few hours?'

'Oh, but now?' She was surprised. 'How can we do that?'

'You've had, what is it?—perhaps two days away since you've come here. Well, why don't we stop hiding from everyone starting right now and just go into Tokyo together?'

'But your wife may come awake,' Saeko protested.

'She's never awake,' he said disgustedly.

'Please, no,' she said. And in a minute she went on, 'Sometimes, I say to myself, whether you like me because she is like that, or whether you like me. Sometimes I say, she will get well and then it will end. This is what you want. Isn't it true?'

He didn't answer her for a long while, thinking it over, and then, long after she might have expected an answer, he muttered, 'No, no, no, Saeko. No. Do you know what I think, Saeko? I think we really are in . . . in love. Dependent upon one another. It's funny, in a way. God, how sick everything is, how rotten. But I don't dare hope for anything. If I hope for her to get over it, I hope to lose you. But I can't hope for her death either, I can't hope that she won't get better, you know. It's sick, but I'd rather have everything go on . . . this way . . . than,' but there was no alternative he could think of which made any more sense than the admittedly senseless preference he was expressing.

Saeko listened closely to what he said, and then frowned and turned from him, putting her arms up, her hands under her head. 'But if I say to you, I love you, I wonder does it mean the same as when you say to me, you love me?'

Ephraim looked over and saw that she was think-ing seriously about the question, and he chose to

112

take her question lightly, as though she wondered only about a matter of translation of her language into his, and he laughed at her. 'And my brother says you aren't attractive!'

'Oh!' She looked at him. 'He says I am ugly?'

'I didn't say that.'

'Well,' she said soon, 'I will say I love you,' and she looked at him again, her thoughtful cast again turning down her brows, 'but I do not know if it means the same.'

Ephraim found he had to laugh each time she tried to be serious about the word *love*, and finally she stopped trying and laughed with him.

14

The month drew to its close too naturally, too easily. Nights ended and days began as they would end and begin for all time, and the pressure of reality made Ephraim discard the meaning of the month even before it ended.

He went to the Tokyo office one day, at an hour when he knew Inders would not be there, and chatted with his former secretary for some minutes. Then he went into the office which Inders now used and took a company cheque and wrote upon the back of it, *Loan,* and made it out to cash, signing it himself. He jammed the cheque into his wallet, left the office and waited for Inders to return.

When Inders finally did come back, Ephraim spoke to him for a time, but said nothing of the cheque. He said only that he meant to write to the company and inform them that things would have to improve before long; it might take a few months, but they could not endure as they were, and had to change for the better. At that time, he was going to seek to enter their employ once more. Until then, Ephraim said, he would never be unaware of his indebtedness to them. He shook Inders' hand and left the office.

He deposited the cheque in his own account and

went home, feeling the heaviness of a new burden replacing one which he had pushed aside. It was the first time he had done such a thing, and even the fact that he had written *Loan* upon the cheque did not decrease the weight of the act. He had made out the cheque for two thousand dollars.

He said nothing of what he had done to Saeko, and was irritable for a few days, and silent all the morning of the day he returned to Tokyo to regain the cancelled cheque. Saeko said nothing about his irritability or his silence, and Ephraim sat nervously in the train as he rode into Tokyo. He was frightened, but knew the urgency of completing the act he had started.

It was completed quite easily. As he had before, he chatted with his secretary for a time, and when the mail came, he sought for cigarettes in his pocket and then asked if the girl would mind running down to get him a package. She leaped to the service, and once she had gone, Ephraim swiftly pulled out the brown packet from the bank, opened it and retrieved the cancelled cheque. He folded it and stuck it into his pocket, sealed the envelope with a few drops of mucilage and replaced the packet into the stack of mail. His secretary returned in only another minute, and Ephraim smiled weakly and opened the cigarettes and took one, but had trouble lighting it because his hand shook. His secretary held a match for him and said, 'You're not feeling well, Mr Rome?'

'No no,' smiled Ephraim. 'I'm all right. Just a little dizzy. But I think I might not wait for Inders.

115

Would you tell him I'll drop in on him perhaps next week?'

Now that he had succeeded, Ephraim was still more frightened by his act. Before, he had known he had a month to repair things, and had failed. From now on, there would be no telling how much time he had.

There was not even time to measure the new burden.

That night, at about midnight, his wife died. Ephraim was dizzy and unbelieving. While she lived, it had been as if she were not there, as if she had resigned her part in life long before; and yet she lived, and had no sickness, and Ephraim had grown accustomed to being annoyed with her. But he had never expected her to stop living. It was nothing more than that: she stopped living.

Ephraim had returned to the room shortly after midnight and had gone to bed, and he lay thinking with terror of what he had done, and then for a time he managed to displace all thinking from his mind. Soon a queer sensation came over him. He knew something was wrong, and looked through the darkness towards his wife's bed. He listened. He left his bed and turned on the light and looked at his wife, but she looked merely as though she slept. He was about to turn off the light, but could not lose the queer sensation that the room was different, and again he went to his wife's bed. It was only then that he realized she was not breathing. He took her hand, which was cool but still with some warmth to

116

it, and he rubbed it, then swiftly sent Saeko to fetch the doctor.

The doctor told Ephraim that his wife was dead. Since there was nothing more to be said for it, the doctor suggested she had died of a broken heart. All he could say beyond that was that, like Nancy, his wife had not wanted to live.

Ephraim was stunned beyond the funeral. The funeral itself was like some lesser sort of ceremony, the taking of flowers to a grave which had long been marked. His wife rested beside Carl and beside Nancy in Yokohama, and Ephraim, attending the lonely affair, felt that his wife was happier now than she had been since Carl's death. He also felt his own aloneness for the first time, felt the fullest impact of the children's deaths for the first time. He now shared the experience alone, and even Saeko could not share it with him.

He had to readjust himself to what seemed an entirely new situation in Akiya. Saeko was somehow remote from him. His wife was gone. He was worried about the money he had borrowed. His walks along the beach and road grew slower, longer, still more morose, and Saeko one evening asked him, 'Do you think you will leave now?'

'Leave now?' Ephraim burst into a kind of laughter he had not known for months. 'Why must I leave now, Saeko?'

'But now you don't have the job, and are alone.'

Ephraim gazed back at her. 'Why am I alone?'

'But you have no family here.'

117

Ephraim considered it and could find no answer to make. She was questioning his devotion to her, questioning it reasonably and kindly, seeming to be asking nothing of him. As stunned as he had been, and as worried about the money he had taken, it was true he was paying less attention to Saeko. Rather than think she, too, was given a new set of circumstances by his wife's death, it only occurred to him that it was unfair of her to expect much attention just after his wife's funeral, and he gave his mind to that rather than to any analysis of his devotion to Saeko.

15

The Autumn persisted and gave no hint of winter, except in the thickening richness of its colours, the deep yellows and browns, the colour-sharpening clarity of daylight, the throbbing lavender-greens of the sea. The days remained warm and the voices of children sang along the beach and the waters, which settled violet to wake up in rose-green iridescence, in quiet vibrancy.

Ephraim was grateful to Saeko for the days she gave him to think, neither suggesting that she should leave, nor that he should rush to her with a renewal of his devotion, and one evening he came to her in her room and talked with her and then broke off the conversation to say, 'Of all the things I know, the thing I know the best is that I don't want to leave this place.'

'But if I leave this place, then,' she said, 'you still stay here?'

'You are this place,' he told her.

'Am I?' She looked down. 'You see, I am glad you will stay, but I want you to say you would stay with me. Because of me only. Because now, I am sorry, you will have a new little child.'

Ephraim lay back to think of what she had said.

Once the news had sunk into all the corners of his brain, he was excited and pleased. It seemed to turn the entire course of his life about, as if the tragic cycle must be completed. Life was now coming in, no longer going out. 'Saeko, is it true?'

'Oh yes,' she nodded. 'I am sorry. I could tell you this weeks ago, but everything is always so sad. Now I must tell you.'

'When?'

'The baby will be in less than six months, I think.'

Ephraim, through his happiness at the news, continued to worry, for the father of the life which was coming in was at best jobless, at worst in considerable trouble with his former employers, and in any event insecure. He glanced over and saw that she was observing not his happiness, only his worry. 'Oh, we'll manage all right,' he told her. 'I have some money . . . saved away, Saeko. It will last. You and I will marry now.'

'Marry? You do not have to marry with me, though.'

'Saeko, can't you see I'm glad about it? I want the baby, I want the baby very badly.'

'Do you really want, then?' She smiled her untelling smile but at a moment when Ephraim knew it meant pleasure. 'Then I am glad.'

'Why, Saeko,' Ephraim said after some moments, 'I used to day-dream that it would be something like this. Once we lost Carl . . . then Nancy . . . and with her like that . . . my God, I . . . do you know? I used to think how sweet it would be, to be here alone with you. This place is very beautiful, and you . . . oh, you're very good.'

She listened contentedly. 'So there will be a baby, and now someday you can forget some of your sadness. You will be able to work and we will live together with children. Is it what you want?'

'Of course,' but Ephraim was also thinking of how long they might live such a life before Inders discovered the loss of two thousand dollars. If they could settle into their new life quickly, provide the appearance of stability rapidly, then he might make an application to re-enter his company's employ before the loss was discovered; but that would be impossible. He was sure there were no flowers, however lovely of themselves, which could grow out of the soil of his tragedies to please his company's executive, who would in any event want him not in Japan but in America.

'No, now you are not happy,' Saeko said nervously, seeming able to read his face as he could determine the meaning of her smiles. 'There is not enough money. Please do not worry. I, too, can work.'

Ephraim wondered what she meant by that. Would she earn five thousand yen towards the maintenance of their family by being a third maid for Americans? That would be still worse than being a bar girl, and a sense of revulsion smashed into his brain. 'Don't be foolish. There is enough money. I have two thousand dollars.'

'Two thousand?'

'About seven hundred thousand yen.'

121

Saeko's eyes widened. 'You are so rich? But with so much money, we can not have to worry for two years, don't you think so? I did not know you were so rich.'

'Well,' he said, then stammered a bit and concluded, 'but it won't last forever, after all. I have to work.'

'Oh, yes. But you will get good job and there is a lot of time.'

'I only meant to say that you mustn't think of working, yourself. Do you understand?'

'I am sorry. You do not want me to work. But I think to do nothing wrong.'

'Whatever kind of work you did would be wrong. Do you understand?'

He wasn't sure she did, but she was silent. Ephraim left the table and walked out on to the beach, standing before the late evening waters of Sagami, staring across at the vanishing silhouette of Fuji's summit. He had wanted to tell her how he came by the money, but was too ashamed to mention it.

The next day he got the idea of writing to New York to tell the executive that his wife had died. Perhaps, seeing that this would be evidence in support of his previous letter—which had said his wife was worse and not able to travel—they might be willing to tender some new leniency towards him. He used his home address and the following week paced nervously during the hour which preceded the coming of the young postman on his bicycle. It was

122

not until the beginning of the week after, that he received his reply.

The company's new letter was as brief and formal as had been its predecessor. They offered him their sincerest condolences on the death of his wife, and scarcely knew what to say after he had suffered the way he had; reading between the few sentences, Ephraim sensed some embarrassment there, as though they had held it somewhat improper for him to write them of his wife's death at all after he had undergone so much already. The second paragraph of the letter suggested that it ought to be unbearable for him to remain in Japan any longer, and if he wished to return at once, they were prepared to give him a position in New York. They hoped to have an affirmative answer within a week. The letter was signed *Sincerely*, and Ephraim tore it up and scattered the pieces across the brown sand of the beach.

Yet, during the next days, darts of what felt like painful reason sped sharply through Ephraim's melancholy, and for brief instants he saw all of the events of the past months hurled together in a fury of enchanted terror: the house, haunted, the rock, Carl, the sullen little girl who died of too little, the wife who lay dead alive until dead of nothing, and there were silvery little bursts of light which intruded upon each scene, which was the curious girl he had stolen from a bar in Shimbashi, from the position of third maid in Meguro-ku, the solace of his infidelity; and the music to it all was the music Carl gave it,

123

for Ephraim could still hear the thin little voice too clearly singing *Toryanse . . . Go through . . . Go ahead . . .* telling Ephraim that life was not a thing from which one turned back. And with those bursts of seemingly rational images upon him, seeing all no more complexly than it really was, it came to Ephraim that he ought to sit down and write the letter to New York, ought to hurry there and work to forget all that had happened to him at Akiya, by sinking deeply, deeply back into the details of the company he knew best; he ought to turn his back on Akiya, Saeko, *Toryanse*, and do anything but go ahead. During those instants, he felt he owed Saeko nothing. She had earned her own reward, had known all along what she was doing, had taken her chances.

But the notions of returning died as soon as the images left him. What cooled his temper were the Akiya evenings, the rapture of the locusts at twilight, and the dawn affairs between the sun and sea, and Saeko herself, who was never, when before him, the girl of his curious bursts of fear; or if she was, he could not realize, when she was before him, that he might not be in her debt, or even that he could want to be away from her and the depth of life she had put about him when all else was falling away lifeless.

One afternoon, just as he endured such fears and imagined he heard Carl's voice singing, he seemed to hear the song outlasting his uncertainties, and then realized he heard the shrilly sweet voices of many children singing from the old wooden building by which he walked—a school building—and

124

they were singing *Toryanse*. He stood listening to them, unable to avoid the impossible feeling that the song was being sung for him, that it still contained some knowledge for him, or that at worst it was a reminder to him of the prison which had closed around him. It was while standing beside the school building, listening, that he saw clearly how pointless it had been to write to his employers at all, and how much more pointless to write now, for what if he did agree to return to America? Still the loss of the two thousand dollars in Tokyo would be discovered. The children sang, '*Ikiwa yoi yoi kaeri wa kowai, Kowai nagara mo, To-oh-ryan-se . . .*'

He returned to the house, resolved to tell Saeko what he had done, how he had stolen the money, to advise her to go away and find someone more dependable than him, realizing that she bore a Eurasian baby in her womb, but perhaps there would be someone, some saint. He couldn't do it. Instead, Saeko brought up the fact that it would be best if they were to leave Akiya soon.

'Please, we must,' she told Ephraim. 'Because if I have baby here, it is no good.'

Ephraim understood.

It was not only apparent that they had to move, but move fairly quickly. Saeko's pregnancy was not yet noticeable to him, but Saeko said that soon it would be clear to women, and before long to everyone. It wouldn't do for them to marry now and have a baby less than six months after his wife's death, and even a more uncomfortable period after the death of Carl, and of Nancy. The very fact that

125

such was the schedule gave Ephraim new reason to vent his shame against himself. How callous he had to be! that he could father a child with a nearly strange girl, upon the deaths of his own children.

His disgust for himself he kept as secret as he could, and he told Saeko he would make plans to find a new house, a new town, soon.

16

That evening he went into Zushi to do some shopping. There was no need for it, but he felt that he had to move about. He bought a pint of whisky among other things, and returned to Akiya, and carried the bag of groceries about with him for a time before going into the house. The evening was one of those which brought him delight and, walking along the sea, he had the feeling he had known while walking there with his wife, after the deaths of the children; he knew that it would be nice to walk there with a clear life and a clear conscience, but as it was the niceness was only a hunger within him.

He went into the house and poured whisky into two glasses, giving one to Saeko, who sipped a bit and then admitted she did not like the taste of whisky.

'Why not?' asked Ephraim, drinking his own whisky hurriedly. 'You were a bar girl, weren't you?' He finished off his glass and poured another.

She took no offense and even giggled. 'But I never like whisky. I was not honest. I always drink only water, but the people pay for whisky. That was how that business works. Don't you know?'

'Yes,' he said, 'I know,' and he swallowed more

whisky. 'Well, I could make you a drink of green toothpaste and water. How about that?'

'That doesn't sound so good,' she said, smiling, still taking no offense.

Ephraim, not knowing why he was trying to hurt her, stopped trying and began to drink silently.

Saeko left the room to make dinner and when she came back she said, 'Today, Mrs Nakano looks at me and I think she thinks something.'

Ephraim was drinking more slowly. 'Yes?'

'Maybe we should move soon.'

'I told you I'd take care of it, Saeko.'

'Where do you think we will go? Have you been looking at some house?'

'Well, it's hard to find a house quite like this one, you know,' Ephraim lay back on the floor. 'You have to learn its history, its ghosts, it wretchedness. I always say, "Has anyone died here recently?" And if the answer is, "No," then I know that house isn't for me. Also, I want one more accessible to the bars of Shimbashi than this one. History has a way of repeating itself, and one should always be prepared. Isn't that right?'

'I don't understand what you say,' she told him softly, as if only now understanding some of the cruelty in his tone.

Instead of answering, Ephraim began to sing, 'Koko wa doko no hosomichi ja . . . Tenjin-sama no hosomichi ja . . .' stumbling over both the words and melody.

'You are a little drunk,' said Saeko. 'I will get you some coffee.'

'Say, you get me Tenjin-sama. How do you call him? Is there a special way of invoking Tenjin-sama? Who the hell is Tenjin-sama?'

'Tenjin-sama is man,' said Saeko. 'Do you really like whisky so that you can drink so much? You have drink nearly the whole bottle. I will make coffee.'

'Yes, I just have a few questions I'd like to ask old Tenjin-sama. Hey,' muttered Ephraim, 'Saeko, Saeko, Saeko, who is the God of Thieves? Who?'

'The God of Where?' asked Saeko, standing by the door.

'Very well then, who is the God of Akiya? Or how does one get straight to the spooks spooking haunted houses? Spirits, Saeko, spirits, spirits as no whisky knows. You know what I think, Saeko, my reason? I'll tell you. If the spirits of former occupants occupy this house, then the spirits of a little boy, my son, of a little girl, my daughter, and of my belated wife —what was her name?—they are all here. Now. Are you frightened, Saeko?'

Ephraim looked over at her and it seemed she really did look frightened. 'You see,' he was going to proceed and create still more ghosts, but then was touched by her concern. 'No,' he said, 'it's a lot of hooey. Do you know what hooey is? It's nothing. That's what hooey is. Saeko, tell me you love me. Western-style.'

'Please let me make coffee now,' she said.

'Western-style,' he went on. 'Now, in the West, we have our special kind of mysteries and romances. We're short on ghosts, but we're long on heroes.

129

We have so many heroes that we don't even care if they're good or bad. In fact, the worse, the better. Nothing better than an evil hero, Saeko. Inspires the ladies. Therefore, if you will please be inspired —Western-style—and say to me . . . here, you put your hands together, really knot them up, and I'll pretend you're wearing gingham . . . so you say, "Oh, Ephraim, Ephraim, you evil man, my heart's only love" . . . can you say that?'

Saeko stared stupidly.

'Yes,' he looked away again, sitting up on the tatami, his legs crossed. 'You say, "Ephraim, you sinner, you stinking sinner, you did it for me, and even though you're evil, I love you because you did it for me. As long as you were being evil for me, beloved evil Ephraim, why didn't you take three thousand? Five thousand? Ten thousand?"' It seemed to him funny and Ephraim began to laugh, then stopped and looked at her and concluded, 'It goes something like that.' He watched her gaping at him, feeling the deadening thickness of whisky in his head. 'Saeko, what will we do? What will you do?'

She came and knelt beside him and pulled at his arm. 'Let me take you to bed.'

'They'll be after me,' he told her, taking her head between his hands and holding it almost roughly. 'They'll take me and you'll be alone, you and the baby. My baby. My life, Saeko. I want the baby, too.'

'No, please don't be like this,' she said. 'You are making me unhappy now. Come to bed. You will sleep, then later we eat.'

'I stole it, Saeko. I stole all of it. They'll find out. I took it and thought I could pay it back, but I stole it. That's what they'll say and they'll be right. I don't know what made me think I should do it. I didn't know what to do.' He held her head and stared into her eyes, and his own eyes were so frenzied that she seemed finally able to see into his words beyond their drunkenness. 'Forgive me, Saeko. All I wanted was to make things work out.'

'Please, I don't understand,' she said, her voice shaking, and she took his hands from her cheeks.

'Damn it, forgive me!' he demanded, taking her now by the shoulders. 'It could have been all I wanted it to be. I didn't know about the baby, I didn't know, but that would only have made it perfect. God, how grateful I would have been for the baby. They'll take me away, Saeko, and what will you do?'

She only stared at him and he finally released her. She sat down on the tatami.

'Saeko, should we run away together? Tomorrow. Let's do that. It's all we can do.'

She sat still for some while and Ephraim, sobered by his confession, sat back and watched her. She stood up at length, leaving the room slowly as she said, 'I will make coffee.'

They lay together that night, neither moving nor sleeping. Ephraim was able to drop off only intermittently, and he woke up with a headache at some hour before dawn and left the bed to stroll out upon the dark and fragrant beach; only the soft splashing of the sea broke against his conciousness. It grew cold and he returned to the house and to Saeko's side, and again slept intermittently until it was light.

They didn't speak in the morning until Saeko had made their breakfast and they sat together over it.

Then she said, 'What you tell me last night. Is it true?'

'Saeko,' he was going to try to explain it, but it was beyond explanation. He nodded. 'Isn't there someplace we could go together?'

'But the people will look for you.'

'Of course, but,' and Ephraim stopped, realizing the insanity of an American trying to hide even as he lived a normal life in Japan. He looked down at the food Saeko had prepared and lost his desire to eat. 'What will you do, Saeko?'

'They will come for you, then?' She seemed unable to take it as a fact that Ephraim had left himself no alternative to punishment as a criminal.

'Sometime they will,' he answered. 'I don't know when.'

'Can't you give the money back?'

'Most of it, yes. But what good would it do?'

'It would be better not to have it, than for you to go away,' she said without looking at him, her voice calm and as untelling as her smile, but again he could judge her by her gestures and even the slightest inflection of her words, and he was too aware of a terrible depth of unhappiness he had brought her.

'You see, I can't simply replace the money. I'd have to give it back. They'd still punish me. At least, they would make me leave the country, go back to America. They'd say it's a part of my illness, they'd have my brother to speak for them, the company, the law. It's no good. Whatever I do, they'll take me away. But Saeko, they owed it to me. They owed me that much help. I only wanted to borrow the money, not to steal it, and after all I've done for them in the past,' his voice fell off.

'Is it true?' she again asked, even more softly.

'And as a criminal, Saeko, I'd never be able to return. I wouldn't be able to take you to America. No, I can't give the money back. We have to risk the possibility that they . . . won't find out. We just have to take what life we have together and,' he picked up his fork and set it down again.

'Then you will leave me,' she said, as if telling herself that this was how it was and only now recognizing it as a fact.

17

Ephraim and Saeko began taking walks together. They walked by the sea and down the road, and people looked at them without obvious suspicion, except for the one lady whom Saeko identified as Mrs Nakano. They walked without speaking, glad to be out in the sunlight and the crisp autumn air.

One morning they walked again by the school building, and it seemed strange to Ephraim that the children should again be singing the song as they passed by, but it was certainly *Toryanse*. He scowled and asked Saeko why the children seemed always to be singing that one song.

'They sing many songs,' said Saeko. 'Perhaps now they sing this song because soon it is *Shichi-go-san*, day for children to go to shrine. *Toryanse* is good song for *Shichi-go-san*.' She seemed sad as she answered and Ephraim wondered if she was thinking of the baby she carried, who might go to the temple without a father, or even a legitimate mother, with even its nationality obscure.

'When my son died,' said Ephraim, 'that is the song he sang.'

'Yes,' said Saeko. 'It is melancholy.'

She was watching the windows from which came the somewhat static voices of the singing children.

134

'I don't know,' Ephraim shook his head. 'I've been thinking, Saeko. I believe I was wrong. We have to take a risk, but maybe we have to take a different risk. We can't live like this, close and apart at the same time, and always wondering what the hell day we spend together is the last day. I'll take the money back. I have nearly all of it. Perhaps Inders will help.'

'Inders? What is this?'

'He's the man who has my job now, damn him. Maybe I can convince him that I was out of my head, that I was crazy. Do you understand? Maybe that's what I must do.'

She shook her head. 'Then you won't come back.'

'But maybe I will, don't you see? And if I do, we wouldn't have to go on like this. Saeko, whatever happens, I'd find some way of helping you. You know that, don't you?'

'You should not go,' she said.

Suddenly, inside the school building, the song came to an end.

Ephraim said it was something he had to gamble, and although Saeko asked him not to go many times, and accused him of wanting to leave her, he took an afternoon train into Tokyo, went to the bank and removed all the money there. He had only ten dollars less than the two thousand he had borrowed.

Stuffing the money into an envelope, he walked from the bank to the office building where he had been employed.

Inders was not in and Ephraim, hot and miserable, sat some moments waiting for him, the envelope fat with dollars in his hand. Soon he got the idea that it would be better if he left the money for Inders with a note; it would be easier writing than speaking of all he had to say.

He got paper from the girl, once his secretary and now Inders', and did his best to write a letter covering the madness which had made him take the money, and assured Inders that he would return the ten dollars at the first opportunity, and that he had left himself with less than the ten dollars. He might even ask Inders for the loan of that twenty he had once been offered, he wrote, and begged Inders to say nothing of the loan, apologizing again and again in the note for his stupidity and madness. He left the note and envelope together with the secretary and rushed out of the building.

He felt freer than he had felt since before the first of his tragedies as he sat in the Second Class car of the Zushi train. He had perhaps two-thousand yen to his name, but felt sure that, however degrading it must be, he could borrow a few dollars here and there from American friends until things picked up. Between a borrowed dollar here and a few thousand earned yen there, they would manage. It seemed to him, too, that Inders would surely have to be decent about what he had done and, even though he was ten dollars short, keep the matter quiet. Ten dollars was, anyhow, less than the twenty Inders had pledged him on occasion. It was reasonable to think that all he had to worry about now was that Inders would be that decent, and it seemed much easier to worry about that than to wait and worry about being dragged away by the Japanese immigration authorities, dragged away from Saeko and the baby who had turned the cycle about, making new life where before life was only being stilled.

Upon returning home, he found Saeko upon her futon, all the reason gone out of her and away from him. She was more lifeless in her appearance than ever his wife had looked. Saeko seemed to have jolted energetically out of life and fallen into an awkward position. Even though she was upon her quilt, there was nothing about her which looked asleep, not even her eyes: they were closed, but it seemed that beneath the lids the eyes were straining to see. Her lips were curled slightly, her arms stretched away in unlikely directions, her legs parted. She looked nearly as if, in death, she was undergoing the labour of childbirth.

Ephraim, seating himself beside her, looked at the tiny square bottle from which she must have extracted her death; upon its label were printed a few *kanji* which he couldn't read. Somehow, the bottle looked familiar and he wondered if he hadn't seen it about the house. He set the bottle down and sought some way of addressing Saeko, to ask her forgiveness or to demand that she return to life, but he could not order even those ideas, and all at once, trembling, he stood and began to shout at the walls of the room: '*Kill! Kill!*'

He walked into the next room and shrieked, '*Kill!*'

He went from room to room and shouted at the walls, at the ceilings, at the floors, addressing what-

137

ever spirits might once have been there or were there forever, 'Kill me! I'm next! Kill me!' until he had shouted himself hoarse. Then he sat upon the floor and wept with his hoarse voice, loudly, furiously.

The room grew dark and he left the house for the sweetness of the sea's cool wind and he sat near the monstrous rock not far down the beach, letting the creeping tide wet his shoes, looking out to the horizon which was being devoured by the night. The sea was black. Down the way and behind him there were other houses, and lights, and Ephraim looked at them and envied them and again he wept, and as he wept he thought most of all of Saeko, who had been his last chance at life.

The night was late and the sea air cold before Ephraim returned to the house. As he passed through the little kitchen, the telephone there rang and he picked up the receiver as if reflexively. It was Inders: 'Rome? Listen, I got your note, of course. And the money. I wanted to thank you very much for your honesty. Jesus, that could have caused me real trouble.' Ephraim muttered, 'It's all right.' 'Rome? I've sent a nightletter off. I didn't spare the words, either. I've tried to describe something of your grief and how mixed up everything has been as best I could, and of course I had to mention the two thousand. Now, the only thing that will come of it, I'm sure, is that they'll want you to go back, and I tell you, it's the only thing for you. You understand? It was a decision I made less for the good of the company than for your own good. You understand that, don't you? . . . Rome? . . . You would have done the same thing for me, and I'd have been grateful.' Ephraim didn't try to understand what Inders was saying and just mumbled, 'Thank you,' and put the receiver back into its cradle.

He went to Saeko's room.

When he had straightened Saeko's body, soothing her eyelids by pressing them softly with his fingers, as if to relieve her eyes from their awful final straining, he sat back on his knees and took up the bottle and opened it, smelling of it; though it smelled vile, it wasn't enough to strengthen his swaying sense of life.

He turned out the light and lay down beside Saeko, their bodies touching, so that they would have no doubt who was the father of the baby, so that there would be that last weak attachment to life: there had nearly been new life and it had been his, and it had been on the verge of springing out of the house at Akiya.